XAVIER

SMOKEJUMPERS

BOOK SIX

BY EVIE RILEY

XAVIER

SMOKEJUMPERS

BOOK SIX

COPYRIGHT © 2024

EVIE RILEY

SECOND EDITION

ISBN: 978-1-77357-676-3

PUBLISHED BY NAUGHTY NIGHTS PRESS LLC

COVER ART BY WILLSIN ROWE

Dear Reader,

When I left off with Gage and Xavier's story, I had originally intended to leave it as it was, BUT so many of you had questions. Now, usually I would have made you wait and I would have answered those questions—mostly about Dexter and the twins, Greyson and Asher, in their own books in due time. Simply because that's typically how things play out in my head and the kids in Gage's book weren't ready for their full on detailed stories yet. I'm a chronological writer, I guess.

Anyway, then I saw that a few of you felt Gage was more of a happy for now kind of ending rather than a happily forever after, and well, I had the idea that I needed to fix that.

So I started working on Xavier, a continuation from where Gage left off, mostly. I did answer some things about the three young men, but not enough to detract me from writing their books later. Yep, more breadcrumbs. Lol

I do so hope you enjoy!

Love,

~Evie Riley

XAVIER

A long-distance relationship.
A lonely home.
The flames burn fiercely when they are together.

Xavier Cruz has just celebrated his one-year sobriety, and he and Dexter are slowly mending their father/son relationship. Will Dex finally reveal his big secret?

Gage Torres is troubled that this may be his first Christmas without his younger brothers. Will the trickster twins have something up their sleeves for Gage again this year?

Living with the love of your life hundreds of miles away is a lonely way to be. Despite all the jet-setting and red-eye flights, it's no longer enough for either man. Something has to give, and soon.

Will the two men survive the long-distance relationship, or will the New Year bring about shocking changes they never could have imagined?

Xavier is a continuation from Gage. Please read Gage first.

CHAPTER ONE

Xavier

"I WANT TO congratulate you all on your success today. This marks the beginning of a new life. A life clean and sober and filled with the many wonderful things that comes with living free and independent of that which used to rule you."

Clapping erupted around the small room, our entire group having been crammed in the small auditorium of the local high school for this ceremony. Our chairman, Robert, smiled at us from the stage while he gripped either side of the podium.

When the clapping finally died down, Robert began to speak again. "Today marks one year. I hope to see you all for our next ceremony to celebrate two years and thereafter. Congratulations, all."

All of this felt so surreal. Even the gold chip in my hand, no matter how many times I turned it over onto its opposite side, still didn't feel real. The ridges carved into the face of it, stating that I was one year sober, were smooth to the touch as I grazed my thumb over it.

Pride filled my chest—at least, that's what I hoped it was. Getting back in touch with my emotions through therapy over the last nine months had been intense, to say the least. I never really had that healthy of a relationship with the deeper parts of myself, and that had become rather apparent and a huge slap in the face when I'd begun to really focus inwardly.

On the one hand, I was glad to have finally started to heal myself. As scary as it was to stop drinking and really focus on getting my mental health back in order, just as Robert had said in his speech, it had been freeing.

On the other hand, my future was uncertain. Sure, I had a great job and a boyfriend that I loved dearly, but there were still things that I was struggling with that felt like once I got a few steps put in front of me, something would come along to send me five steps back from where I started.

Namely my son, Dexter.

"Hey." Someone clapped me on the shoulder, bringing me out of my funk. "They're serving pizza and wings, you want me to bring you a plate?"

Danny, my one friend from AA, was giving me a toothy grin while waiting for my answer. He was a bit younger than me, had lost his way after his wife and daughter had died in a horrific car accident that had left him severely scarred on the right half of his body.

Pain killers to numb his injuries had soon turned into a full blown addiction that he'd eventually swapped for alcohol because it was cheaper and easier to get. Unfortunately, it was a tale as old as time and one I knew all too well how it went.

I was glad that someone like Danny, who radiated practical sunshine out of his ass, had found his own light in coming to AA and getting himself clean. That was a man that I could admire.

"Nah, I'm good." Standing, I tucked my chip into my pocket. "I've actually got to head to the station. To save lives and whatnot." That last part was partially a joke, but one Danny found absolutely hilarious nonetheless.

He clapped me again on the shoulder. "All right, then I'm taking your portion of the wings."

"Go for it. But don't call me at ten o'clock tonight complaining of heartburn."

He let out a gasp. "I'd rather down an entire bottle of pepto than call your cranky ass."

That brought a smirk to my face.

At least my reputation preceded me, even here.

Waving at him, I headed out before anyone else could trap me in a long and drawn out conversation about our hopes and dreams now that we all had our one year chips. I had set goals for myself long before this, and while they were all still a work in progress, I was managing.

Once I shoved the door to the outside world open and stepped out into the fading sunlight, I let myself finally breathe. It wasn't that being in there with a bunch of other recovering addicts made me anxious or anything—quite the opposite, in fact.

But too much of being crammed inside of a tiny room with only one way out had me wanting to crawl right out of my damn skin.

I supposed it was a part of my military training not to want to be trapped in an environment like that. Too many factors played into getting fucked if an enemy were to attack and block off the only line of exit. Or, if for some tragic reason, a fire or something similar were to break out and panic ensued—not much could be done fighting against twenty other people scrambling to get away.

Even now that I was out and a civilian like the rest of society, it was hard to shut that part of my brain off. No matter what I did, my therapist had reassured me—or rather, doomed me?—that I'd always have that gut instinct to survive and get out.

That intuition was what had saved me while in the military, after all.

Shaking my head to rid myself of the thoughts before I delved too far down *that* rabbit hole, I pulled out my cell and scrolled through my text threads, coming upon Gage's. Opening up my camera, I snapped a quick photo of my chip and sent it over to him.

Despite the time difference, he responded almost immediately.

Congratulations, Baby! I'm so proud of you!

There was a smattering of emojis after that, ranging from confetti cannons to hearts.

Damn, I missed him.

Horribly.

Since coming back from Louisiana, I'd had the worst withdrawals from him. Not just because of the lack of sex—which we were more than making up for through texts and phone calls every night—but because I missed *him*. His presence. His energy. His body wrapped up in mine as we fell asleep together.

XAVIER

I'd only had such a short window with him in Louisiana that even now, almost ten months later, it still didn't feel like enough. Our time difference made it complicated to connect with each other at decent times, and our jobs weren't helping that either.

As proud as I was of him for passing his exam and getting into the field of his dreams, I fucking wanted to rip him right out of Louisiana and smuggle him back here to be with me.

Would I ever tell him any of this shit?

Fuck no.

He didn't need to be worrying about my slow spirals into insanity while trying to deal with his own full plate.

Besides, most nights after we said goodnight and hung up, I was good. It was only those few times throughout the month, those one or two nights, that were absolutely fucking diabolical on my mental health. And waking up to an empty bed on top of that when I finally came to was worse than if I just simply jumped off the nearest roof.

While still looking down at my phone, an alert went off that made my heart lurch in my chest.

REMINDER: Dex dinner

Oh, fuck.

Checking the time, I spun on my heel and ran to my truck.

CHAPTER TWO

Xavier

"YOU'RE LATE," WAS all my son said to me the second I sat down in the booth across from him. He had his nose already buried in his menu, a drink half gone with pearls of condensation rolling down the side of the glass and creating a pool on the table.

Wincing, I slipped my jacket off of my shoulders and shoved it into the corner of my side. "Sorry, kid. I got over here as fast as I could."

He wasn't looking up from the menu as I talked. Not even a subtle shift in his brow that indicated he was listening to me. Just his eyes darting over the menu while he scanned it, looking for something to eat.

I loved my kid a lot but sometimes he was difficult to read. Actually, scratch that. He was like a fucking dictionary in a foreign language and I was the idiot trying to translate it.

"Dex?"

He sighed and looked up. "Yeah?"

"I'm sorry."

His face finally faltered, going from that neutral expression to an actual frown. I knew he was upset, even if I was only a couple minutes late. We'd been working on this relationship between us for a couple of months and it seemed that the more I got to know him, the more walls he'd been throwing up lately.

My therapist was adamant that it was Dexter's way of trying to gain control of the situation. I'd been out of his life for a long time, no thanks to his mother. But the logistics of that weren't all that important.

At least not at this stage.

He was a child still, even at the cusp of turning eighteen, and his view of the world was still small. Giving him the space to express himself, no matter if it was happiness or disappointment at me, was what was going to be the thing that would help him in starting to trust me.

I just had to trust the process and not be impatient.

But fuck was it hard not to reach over and pull him into a tight hug and promise him the damn world. He was my pride and joy, my baby, my everything. Losing him had been what hurt the most back then.

The PTSD from the military had only compounded my depression and spiraled me into a person that I barely recognized whenever I got the courage to look in the mirror. A year ago, I'd been a man that was incapable of being there for my son, no matter how much I'd tried to convince myself otherwise.

Here, today, I wanted to prove that old me wrong.

Leaning back in my seat, I slipped my hand into my pocket and pulled out my chip. It made a rough sound as I slid it across the table toward him, the light overhead catching the gold plating that made the thing shine nicely.

He stared down at it, his eyes widening a little bit.

"I was at my meeting to accept my chip," I explained, smiling. "I wanted to get it before our dinner to give it to you."

"Me?" he said, incredulously.

"Yeah, Dex. I want you to know how serious I am about all of this. I know that I wasn't... I haven't been there for you in the past, and trust me, I regret every single second of it, but this is hopefully a small step in proving to you that I'm going to do everything I can to make it up to you. I want to *be* there for you."

He swallowed, his Adam's apple bobbing while he carefully picked up the chip. He rotated it in his hand a few times, much like I had back at the meeting. "One year, huh…"

"Yup."

He was quiet for another moment. "That's pretty impressive."

Grinning, I said, "Just wait until I get my ten year one. I hear that it's *real* gold."

He glanced up at me. "Ten years?"

I could tell by the way that he said that it was laced with hope and mixed with a little bit of skepticism. I could work with that, though. I could prove to him that I was going to keep this thing going. We had the rest of our lives together, and like hell I was going to screw it up any further.

When Dexter slowly set the chip down, he pulled in a deep breath. "Can I talk to you about something?"

My heart stuttered in my chest. "Yeah, of course. Anything."

I hoped it was about whatever had

happened to him that he'd been refusing to talk about. While I didn't want my kid to have to relive any kind of trauma that he might have endured, I knew from experience that getting it out was the first step in recovering from it.

Talking about horrible experiences, even through therapy, had taken a lot out of me. But now with nine months under my belt, that weight that had been settled on my shoulders for so long was slowly beginning to get lighter and lighter as the days passed.

I wanted that for Dexter, too. He deserved that. Suffering with whatever he was keeping locked inside himself would eventually eat away at him like it had me. We Cruz boys had been cursed with that prideful sense of self that made it almost impossible to open up about our deepest darkest secrets.

Even to our own family.

"So, I've been applying to colleges," he said, focusing his gaze back down at the chip on the table.

Okay, not exactly what I was expecting. But hey, at least he was opening up to me about something.

"And," he went on. "I got accepted into one for an early admissions."

My jaw dropped. "Dex, that's amazing! Congratulations!"

His smile was a little worn when he finally looked at me again. "The problem is that it's kind of far away."

Oh fuck.

"How far away are we talking?"

Please don't say on the other side of the damn world.

I'd only just gotten him back. Having

to say goodbye after only a year would fucking wreck me.

"Louisiana," he said slowly.

My body all but collapsed back into my booth, relief practically jello-ifying my damn bones. Oh thank fuck. I could handle Louisiana. "Where abouts?"

"Baton Rouge."

That's near Gage.

"Mom know yet?"

Dexter shook his head.

Interesting.

I wondered why he wasn't telling Kate. Maybe he was afraid she wasn't going to let him go, or try to talk him into going to a local school here. Having a mom like her, one that was steadfast in her beliefs and convictions, could be both a blessing and a curse.

She'd kept him safe all these years,

but she'd also kept him away from many things—namely me—by doing so. It wasn't healthy to raise a child, let alone a boy, locked in a bubble. It created too much confusion once they were thrust into the real world. And while I had no doubts my son was a smart boy, he was also naive to a fault.

"I actually have a friend out that way," I said.

Calling Gage a 'friend' put a sour taste in my mouth. I'd been careful in tiptoeing around the 'boyfriend' talk with Dex, not wanting to freak him out too much by shoving all of my personal affairs down his throat.

It had been hard not to talk about my personal life with him, especially since hiding things from him felt wrong, especially about a relationship.

That wasn't something I was sure about, though. With Kate raising him in the church, I wasn't sure how deeply ingrained her beliefs—and his—were. So pushing the subject didn't seem fair game at this point.

In the future, definitely. But for now, I wanted to focus on our dynamic.

Dexter nodded slowly, tapping his fingers absently on the table. "I wanted to go on a campus tour before I accepted."

He was obviously telling me all of this for a reason. With his mother not involved in any of this, that meant that I had fair dibs. "You want to take a trip out there? I'm sure we could crash at my friend's place."

His eyes lit up. "Really?"

God, he reminds me of when he was a baby.

Blinking back the sudden tears that prickled at the corners of my eyes, I said, "Yeah, of course. Why don't I talk to him and figure out a good time to fly us out. We'll tour the campus and make a weekend of it."

For once, Dexter actually looked excited. "I'd love that."

Pride bloomed in my chest for the second time today. I really hoped this was the beginning to us finally bridging the gap between us.

CHAPTER THREE

Gage

"YOU'VE BEEN STARING at your phone like you're waiting for a dick pic," came a familiar voice from behind me.

Turning to look over my shoulder, I threw Quinn a glare. "Funny. Can't I be happy that my boyfriend's texting me?"

He smirked while ripping the door to his locker open and shoving his dirty shirt inside. "Not much *texting* going on, I see."

He was such a turd, sometimes. Especially since getting together with Jase. Thankfully, that man had softened out more than any of us could've ever imagined. Before they'd gotten together, they were like oil and water.

Though, I guess that came with the territory when one party used to bully the other in high school.

"He got his one year chip," I said, showing off the picture on my phone."

Quinn's eyes softened. "Hey, man. That's great. Sorry, I wasn't trying to be a dick. I was only ragging on you because you've been distracted all day. I don't think I've ever seen you take a boot to the face like that."

I snorted at the memory of Mark slinging his turn-outs at me while climbing out of the fire truck. The damn thing had caught me right on the side of the head, too. Thankfully, the tread was thick enough that it'd bounced right off without leaving much of a dent behind, but damn was it embarrassing.

Quinn was right, though. I'd been distracted since this morning when I'd woken up to Xavier telling me he was on his way to his AA meeting to celebrate his one year. Pride didn't even begin to cover it on how I felt about him accomplishing something so massive. He'd been working so hard on himself over the past year since quitting drinking.

That chip was more than just a small token. It was a symbol that he'd gone and done that damn thing, changing his life for the better. Meeting him and learning about his drinking had been tough. Especially seeing him as the kind of soul that didn't deserve to suffer the way he had in life.

Sure, he'd messed up plenty, but *no one* deserved to go through that shit.

"It's all good," I said, swinging my leg over to the other side of the bench I'd been sitting on for the past twenty minutes. My ass was numb as I stood, making the pins and needles in my leg feel hot. Slapping my ass cheeks a few times did nothing, either.

Guess I just had to ride it out.

Quinn grinned at me. "Hey, you hear about the Christmas party Captain Clarke's making us throw? I totally put Jase on the planning committee."

"You wrote him in?" I tsked and shook my head. "How cruel. You know he can't decorate for shit."

He let out a roarous laugh. "Yeah,

that's the point. Come on, I have to pick on him somehow. It's what keeps our sex life alive."

That had me rolling my eyes. Leave it to Quinn to keep up with the light negging. I swear, you could take a man out of high school but you couldn't reform a former bully completely. At least these pranks were much more tame compared to the shit Jase was put through back when he was a kid.

"It's all in good fun, I swear." Quinn lifted his hands up on either side of his head.

"What are you two asswipes talking about?" Jase was walking into the locker room, shedding his shirt that was soaked in sweat. The hair on his chest, normally wiry and curly, was pressed down on his clammy skin.

"Apparently he signed you up for the decoration committee for our Christmas party," I said, smirking when Quinn threw me a glare for ratting him out. I was nothing if not the occasional pot stirrer.

"Really," Jase drawled, looking over at his boyfriend. He grabbed the other man by his waist, slamming him back against the lockers and pinned him there with his body. "Do I have to teach you a lesson in behaving, Sanders?"

Quinn let out a breathy laugh when Jase reached around and slapped his ass cheek, holding it in a firm grip. "I mean... I wouldn't mind."

Rolling my eyes, I slammed my own locker shut. These fucking horn-dogs. "Can you two get a fucking room?"

At this point, they were completely ignoring me in favor of Jase running his tongue up Quinn's neck while the other man let out a slutty moan. It annoyed me more than it should have—okay, maybe I was kind of jealous now that I thought about it.

With my significant other on the other side of the damn country, watching these two assholes get it on was giving me a serious case of blue balls. Don't get me wrong, phone sex with Xavier and sending him sassy pictures throughout the day was all fine and good but it was nothing compared to the real thing.

I craved having him pressed up against me, his dick pounding into me while I begged for mercy. Replicating that with a dildo didn't exactly suffice much anymore, no matter how many sweet words Xavier whispered to me on the other end of the phone.

Bypassing the two lovebirds, I strolled out into the fire station, spotting Ellie over by the bulletin board. "That for the party?"

She flicked her hair over her shoulder, the pen in her hand tapping her clipboard in quick succession. "Yeah. Cap wants us all to pitch in for something. I'm thinking a potluck."

"I'm not much in the ways of the kitchen, so as long as you're good with store-bought, I'm down."

She turned and narrowed her eyes at me. "What *kind* of store bought?"

"Uh... the normal kind?"

Ellie rolled her eyes. "Earth to Gage. You have to at least make to *seem* homemade."

Oh.

"Then from Krista's Scratch Kitchen

down the street."

She grinned. "Excellent. I'll put you down for being in charge of the main course."

What the hell?

She trotted off to find her next victim, leaving me standing by the bulletin board like a complete dumbass. Such was the way of Ellie, though. She was always such a little viper that you didn't realize bit you until much too late.

That was also part of her charm, though.

"She get you, too?" Carmen asked, wandering over.

"Yeah. You?"

She laughed. "Oh yeah. By the end of today, she'll have everyone signed up on the damn list."

Just as I was about to hit her back

with another comment about Ellie, my pocket buzzed. Digging my phone out, I was expected to see Xavier's name pop up, but to my surprise, it was Asher's.

Excusing myself from our conversation, I ducked out the left door of the firehouse and out the back alley where it was much more quiet.

"Hey, you, long time no talk."

"Yeah, sorry about that," Asher said. "Wanted to call in and check on you."

"Worried I took a nasty fall and couldn't get up?"

I could hear the grin in his voice as he said, "You caught me, old man."

I rolled my eyes.

Little shit.

My brothers *loved* picking on my age despite them being not so far behind me. Now that they were both nineteen, they were going to get a nice little dose of reality once they got up to be my age and *their* bones were beginning to creak every time they rolled out of bed.

"Ha, ha. Very funny."

"I know. Poor, Grey. I got the smarts and the humor."

Smirking, I quipped back. "But not the beauty."

He let out an offended gasp. "Rude. I'm taking you off my Christmas card list."

"Hey, now. Don't be saying that. You're coming home for Christmas, mister."

There was a weird pause on the other end of the line. One that I didn't like at all. "Well..."

Uh-uh, no way. This was *not* happening. My baby brothers were both going to come home to me for the holidays because I wasn't going to be taking any other excuse other than an act of god. They'd been away from home long enough to give me grays every time I looked in the damn mirror by being out in the world without me.

If I was about to spend a holiday by myself—my first holiday *without* them—I was going to fucking lose it. Xavier was going to have to commit me to the nearest psych ward.

"Ash, don't you dare," I warned.

"It's just... my boss is kind of being a hardass and wants me to stay through the holidays."

I wanted to groan. This fucking boss of his was not only messing with me reuniting with my brother after him being gone for almost an entire fucking year, but was slowly worming his way into Ash's life in more ways than what I was comfortable with.

To me, it was becoming increasingly obvious that my little brother's crush on the man was going from juvenile puppy love to something that was full-blown. How deep it really was, I had no idea. Asher wasn't exactly chatty on the subject. But the unspoken shit said plenty as it was.

"Ash, you're coming home." My tone was firm. There was no option of him telling me 'no'. I'd fly out to Texas and drag his sorry ass back home kicking and screaming if I had to.

"We'll see," was all he said to that.

"I mean it, Ash. You and Grey are coming home for the holidays."

"Do we get to meet this infamous Xavier if we do?"

"Seriously?"

"What?" Asher's voice flipped from challenging to all innocent. "Come on. You talk about him enough whenever we call. Isn't Christmas the perfect time to introduce us?"

I had a funny feeling that was the original reason for my brother calling. If Greyson hadn't put him up to it first, then they definitely conspired together. I'd been slowly working my way into introducing Xavier into their lives with small mentions here and there about him whenever they called me.

It wasn't much, sure, but I wasn't completely leaving them in the dark about it, either. I wanted my brothers to get to know my boyfriend, even if he was across the damn country. At some point, I *would* actually like for us all to meet and hang out, mostly so I could get a read on whether my brothers approved or not.

It sounded silly to want that from two nineteen year olds when I was well into my adulthood and didn't need their approval in the slightest. However, it would also mean a lot to me, too. My history of dating had never been stellar in the past, with me hardly bringing anyone home on top of that.

Certainly not to meet my brothers.

So doing this with Xavier meant a lot. *He* meant a lot to me. I loved that man and hopefully, eventually, my brothers would, too.

"How about I think about it and get back to you," I finally said.

Asher made a small noise. "Fine. I'll get back to you about Christmas, too."

"Tell your boss that if he doesn't give you time off, he's going to find me on his doorstep."

He huffed. "Fine."

"I love you, Ash."

"Yeah, yeah. I love you, too. Greyson should be calling later."

I flipped my wrist up to check my watch; I had about an hour before that happened. With Greyson already having graduated boot camp and started on his specialized training, that typically ended around five and dinner was at six.

"Got it, thanks."

After ending our call, I pulled my phone away from my ear and stared down at the log. As much as I hassled my brothers, I did mean what I said about seeing them. They could play it off as a joke all they wanted but when push came to shove, they were mine.

We were brothers in name, but

honestly, they were practically my kids. I'd raised them proudly, despite my struggles in doing so over the years. Them leaving the nest and becoming successful was a testament to what I'd sacrificed in order to cultivate them into the young men they'd become.

It hurt, of course, them leaving me behind to go spread their wings and fly. But damn if I wasn't proud, too.

Pulling up Xavier's text thread, I shot him a quick message about a phone call later before heading back into the station.

Hopefully, my brothers weren't going to give me any more grief about coming home.

Because if I had one thing going for me, it was following through with my promises.

CHAPTER FOUR

Xavier

PLANNING A TRIP to a different state would've looked a lot different if I wasn't also simultaneously trying to do it behind my ex's back.

Was it fucked of me to be doing this without Kate knowing?

Probably. But this was the first time since reconnecting with Dexter that he was allowing me in on something she wasn't a part of. Throwing my precautions to the wind was going to be my only solution to this.

I couldn't let this golden opportunity be flushed down the proverbial toilet the second it'd been presented to me. I had to make this perfect, to show Dexter that he could trust me and that I could handle his shit.

Our conversation about him dealing with whatever demons he had in him still rung through my head to this day. I wondered every night before I went to bed what kind of shit my kid had been put through to create that destroyed look on his face when he'd admitted he couldn't deal with my shit on top of his.

My desperation to know was only in an effort to fix it for him. To create the safe space he needed in order to talk to him about what happened. I wasn't willing to jump to any conclusions just yet, but damn if my mind didn't race every time I thought about it.

Hopefully, this trip would change things.

My phone lit up from where I'd tossed it onto my desk, Gage's name scrolling on it. Smiling, I put him on speaker and continued to click through flights.

"Hey, baby."

He let out that familiar soft chuckle of his. "Hey. Got your message. That's exciting about Dexter."

"You okay with us crashing at your place? I can grab a hotel if not. No worries."

He groaned into the speaker. "I swear to god if one more person ditches me, I'm going to scream. No, you're coming here and staying with me. This house is so fucking empty."

Frowning, I leaned back from my keyboard and swiped the phone off of the desk. "What's going on?"

It wasn't like Gage to sound that torn up about something. He'd been fine texting me throughout the day.

So what changed to put him in such a sour mood?

"The fucking twins aren't *sure* if they want to come home for the holidays." The tone in Gage's voice, while sounding annoyed, was laced with despair.

My man was in the middle of a full-blown meltdown. Or, well, as much of a meltdown as Gage could possibly be spiraling into. That man was the most stable person I'd ever met.

"Hey, I'm sure they didn't mean it like

that." Hopefully, my voice was soothing. "They're just being teenagers. Trust me, I have one of my own."

"You know what Asher said to me? That his boss isn't going to give him the vacation days. And then Greyson said that he might be tied up with taking another specialized course to get certified for who fucking knows what."

Not being able to help it, I smiled a little. As sad as it was to hear how cut up about this Gage was, he had a very unique way of ranting about things. He was a charming man who was constantly keeping me on my toes, no matter what we talked about.

Even during sex, I was always tuned in to what that mouth of his was doing.

"Too bad I can't call them to scold them," I teased.

"Would you?"

Rolling my eyes, I said, "No, Gage. They don't even know me."

"So?"

Poor thing. He sounded desperate. I honestly doubted that the boys would actually ditch him for the holidays. More likely than not, they were planning something and trying to throw Gage off their trail. From the stories that I'd heard about them from Gage, that's how they seemed to act.

I could be wrong, obviously, but then again I was more willing to believe that then I would about them being cruel and simply ditching their brother over a holiday meant to bring families together.

Gage had raised those boys better than that, and if the day came that they *weren't* showing up on my boyfriend's door with fucking bows on top of their heads claiming to be Gage's Christmas present, I really would call them up and rip them a new one.

My kid had an excuse to put some distance between us. Gage's did not.

"Baby."

He grunted at me in response.

"It'll work out. I'm going to come keep you company soon."

That seemed to perk him right up. "Oh yeah? What kind of company?"

Oh, that familiar husky tone sent shivers racing up my spine. I loved when he slipped into that.

Leaning back in my chair, the thing creaking under me as I did so, I quickly worked the button above my fly apart and slipped my hand under the waistband. My dick was already half hard, perking right up the moment Gage had called.

My body was so attuned to him that it could predict the man's phone calls. Like a damn satellite radar type shit. I probably needed to be way more concerned about that than I was, but honestly, I couldn't bring myself to care.

"The kind where I wrap my lips around that hard cock of yours," I said.

He groaned instantly. "Oh fuck."

I stroked my cock lazily while I pulled it out of my pants. The tip was already wet with precum, glistening slightly in the dim lighting of my office. Curling a hand over the already swollen knob, I smeared the slick fluid down along my shaft, working myself nice and good while Gage's breathing turned heavy on the other end of the phone.

"Fuck, baby," he said, his voice getting

chopped up for a second while he was readjusting himself. "I want you so damn bad."

"Want to know what else I'm going to do to you once I get my hands on you?"

"Yes," hc groaned again.

"I'm going to lick the tight little hole of yours until you're screaming at me to let you come. You'll be squirming and begging me while I tease you until you can't take it anymore."

His breathing became labored, the telltale sign of him already touching himself. "Mmmm."

"I'm going to fuck you with my tongue and make you come all over your stomach. Then I'm going to lick you clean until you're hard again." Squeezing my own cock was painful, my own dirty talk and imagining Gage under me was already getting me going.

Spreading my legs more, I gave myself room to reach down into my pants and cup my balls, already swollen and tight with my need to come. I couldn't just yet, not until I had Gage right where I wanted him.

"Baby..." He whimpered.

"My cock is going to fit perfectly in that tight hole of yours, isn't it?"

"Yes," came his quick reply. "Yes. It will."

"I'm going to fuck you so deep that you feel it in your belly. I'll fill you with so much cum that you'll explode once I pull out." My hand moved back up to my shaft, rubbing around the sensitive head again as it leaked more precum. "You'd like that, wouldn't you?"

His only response was to whimper

again.

Perfect.

"Once I get you nice and full, I'm going to make you come. Just by telling you to. You'll behave and come for me, won't you, Gage?"

"Ohhh fuck. Yes, I will."

"I want to see it."

The other end of the phone dropped instantly, causing me to blink and pull it back from my ear in disbelief. Before I could even move my thumb over to hit the 'call back' button, a video call appeared on my screen.

Oh, that dirty dog.

Grinning, I answered it. "Show me."

He already had his camera flipped to his crotch where he had his hand gripped tightly around his cock. Fuck, I missed having that thing in my mouth. It was the perfect size and length to suck on. Teasing Gage with it was even more fun.

He'd accused me of having an oral fixation at one point, and honestly, he wasn't wrong.

"Look what you do to me," he growled.

His cock spurted out some precum, drawing a gasp out of him. The camera shook while he tried to keep it steady with the pleasure that was clearly overwhelming his system.

"Keep going, baby. Let me see." My gaze was glued to the screen, my mind no longer focused on getting myself off.

He pumped himself a few times, rolling his palm over his tip with each one and smearing whatever drooled out the tip with each stroke. He was naked on his bed, his legs spread out widely with his feet planted on the mattress while he touched himself.

I wished I was there in the room with him. I'd love to reach out and grab his thigh while he continued to touch himself. Or stroke his hair while watching him come.

My cock ached at the thought.

"Oh, I'm gonna come..." he moaned.

"Come for me, Gage."

His hand sped up, blurring in the camera. His hips bounced while he fucked up into his hand, coming completely undone with just my simple instructions.

"Oh fuck... oh fuck!" He gasped right before cum began spurting out of him like lava, spreading all over his hand and onto his belly. The camera shook along with him.

Setting my phone down for a second while he recovered, I tightened the hold on my own dick and began to move it again. With quick flicks of my wrist, the sounds of Gage's labored breathing sending me right over the edge, I came hard and fast in my own hand, doubling over as the pleasure raced up my spine.

"*Fuck*," I ground out.

"Mmm," Gage let out a slow breath. "Damn, that was good."

I grabbed my phone again just in time to see him lean up and snag a tissue off of the nightstand table next to his bed. While he cleaned himself up, I couldn't help the undying want in my heart that screamed I should be doing that.

I should be the one to clean up my lover after us getting down and dirty. Instead, I was across the damn country with my own rapidly deflating dick in my hand and no one to cuddle up next to and fall asleep with.

Where was the justice in that?

Going into this, I knew long distance wasn't going to be fun. I'd heard horror stories throughout the years of gay guys my own age trying to find love online and the trials and tribulations that went with it.

Did some of those love stories work out in the end?

Of course.

I wanted Gage and I to be a success story, too. But damn if this whole thing wasn't weighing on me.

Our trip out to him was going to be nice, but for the majority of it, I was going to be spending it with my son—rightfully so. Flying us out only for me to get wrapped up in my boyfriend was a ticket to Dexter *never* trusting me again with something that he clearly held so close to his heart.

Something that he'd trusted *me* with and not his mom. That shit mattered.

Regardless of what my own feelings were with the situation between Gage and I, I wasn't going to fuck this up. For the sake of my son, I couldn't.

"Xavier?"

Snapping out of my thoughts, I righted my phone to see that Gage had flipped his camera around. He was so beautiful, even with him looking like his brains had just been fucked out.

"Yes?"

"You okay?" he asked. "You got kind of quiet."

"Just missing you."

He smiled sweetly. "Awww, he misses me."

"See what you do to *me?*"

"I kind of like that lovesick face you've got on," he teased.

"It's only for you."

"Wow, I'm special, huh."

You sure as fuck are.

"You really okay with me and Dex coming to stay with you?"

"Yes. Please. I need the company. I swear, I'll try and keep my hands to myself when your kid's around."

"I like that you said 'try' and not 'will do'."

"Hey, I'm just being honest!"

Shaking my head, I grabbed my own tissue and cleaned myself up before tossing it in the trash and pushing back from my desk. Today had been a long day, and not just from my conversation with Dexter or my AA meeting.

In general, I was exhausted. And why that was, I still wasn't really sure. At this point, I was chalking it up to getting old, or missing Gage—both of which were most likely simultaneously true.

He was a beacon of light that I sought after in the darkness. He breathed life into me when I otherwise couldn't possibly go on. There were things that he'd done to me that he'd never know, ways he'd changed me and molded me into a better person that I'd never ever forget.

I was so glad that I didn't recognize the man in the mirror anymore. This version of me was different from my old one. A new shell having been born that I was excited to get to know.

"I love you," I sighed into the phone, flopping down onto my bed as soon as I reached it.

He laughed. "I love you, too, Xavier. You should probably get some sleep. Let me know about those flights and I'll rearrange my schedule."

"Will do."

CHAPTER FIVE

Xavier

OVER THE NEXT few days, I'd gotten a solid plan together for traveling to Louisiana. With our housing secured for the weekend, all I needed to do now was somehow get in contact with Kate and get her to agree to let me take him for the weekend.

I had a feeling it was going to be an uphill battle with that one. Knowing my ex-wife, she was going to fight tooth and nail on keeping me from taking him anywhere, especially without her present.

So far, she'd been letting us see each other infrequently. I had a guess that she was only doing it because Dexter was turning eighteen soon and that meant he was going to come and seek me out regardless of her own personal thoughts on the matter.

But whatever her reasoning for her giving up a bit of control was, I wasn't going to question it. I'd take what I could get at this point.

Going the easy route and getting Dexter to talk to her for me *was* an option. However, getting him involved in my and his mom's personal affairs, or what we had left of them, left a sour taste in my mouth. He'd already been honest in telling me that our shit was too much for him to deal with.

Respecting that boundary he'd set up needed to happen for me to stay on his good side.

So, that left me with one other option.

I dialed her number and listened as it rang twice.

"Hello?"

Shit, why was I so nervous?

Speaking to my ex after all these years should not be causing my palms to sweat. We literally shared a kid together—there was no reason for me to feel like hanging up the phone and walking around the block to burn off my sudden excess energy.

"Kate, it's me."

There was a long, drawn out pause on the other end of the phone. One that had me pulling my cell back from my ear to check to make sure the call hadn't disconnected. The numbers were still ticking on by, though.

"Kate?" I said.

"How the hell did you get this number?"

Sighing, I said, "It was in the court documents. I figured you never changed it."

"What the hell could you possibly want, Xavier?"

All right, I really didn't appreciate the hostility. I got that I fucked up in the past and broke her heart, but goddamn. After fifteen years, you'd think she would've let sleeping dogs lie.

"I'm calling about Dex."

There was another drawn out pause that wasn't as significantly long as the last, but still enough that it made me antsy the longer it went on. "And?"

"I want to take him on a trip." Dancing around the subject was hard considering I still wasn't sure if Dexter had told her about him getting accepted into college.

He hadn't said anything to me since our dinner a few days ago, so I was going to act under the assumption that he hadn't. I had a feeling he was waiting to tell her before he toured the campus. There was no sense in getting her wound up if he wasn't even sure he wanted to go to Baton Rouge in the first place.

Kate's influence over Dex, while he probably hated to admit it, was a lot. She was still his mom, after all. No matter how many times he'd told me that her neuroticism had weighed on him over the years, her opinion still mattered.

In the end, Dexter was searching for her approval. That's just how it went with your parents.

"Where?" was all she asked.

"Louisiana."

"What the hell could possibly be in Louisiana that you'd want to take my son there?"

My jaw ached from how hard I clenched my teeth at that.

"*Our* son, Kate."

"Don't start with me."

Jesus, fuck. This is precisely the reason why I was hesitant in calling her. No matter how I approached any of this, she was going to come at me combatively. I could try prancing around and sprinkling fairy dust in her face while trying to ask for her permission and she'd still see the devil in me.

"I'm not starting shit, Kate. I'm being honest and trying to communicate with you. He's my son, too. I want to go on a trip with him before he's off to college and we hardly hear from him."

She scoffs. "You mean *you'll* hardly hear from him."

"I meant what I said. How often did either of us talk to our parents once we graduated high school?" The silence on the other end was all I needed to hear to know I hit the nail right on the head. "He's a teenager, he's going to want to go out and make friends and have fun. He's not going to have time to talk to either of us every day. Let me take him on a vacation for a weekend before he leaves me in the dust."

"I'm not comfortable with that."

"Why not?"

"Because I don't trust you. How do I know you're not going to take him to some... strip club? Or some gay bar and force him to drink?"

The paranoia in her voice was prominent. Normally, I'd be rolling my eyes and telling her to shove it. Realistically, I *did* want to do that. However, the true fear laced in her voice was what held me back from doing so.

Kate's religious upbringing had been a contentious point in our relationship up to a point. I'd let a lot of stuff go, especially with my in-laws, on account that I'd been hiding my true self from everyone and blending in had made it easier to deny myself.

She'd never been pushy with her beliefs back when we were dating and only had been a little more so after we'd had Dexter. There was never a point where I considered her to be a zealot, not in the way that her parents were, at least.

So, it was sad to see her—or rather, hear her—acting like this. What I did to her back then had clearly broken her. I'd never be able to make it up to her, no matter how many times I tried to apologize to her or explain how much it had killed me to hide my true self from the world.

What did it matter in the grand scheme of things, anyway?

She'd walked in on the most devastating situation that could ever be imagined. She'd gone from being in a happy relationship as a wife and mother, to being a divorcee and a single mom.

That shit was fucked on so many levels and my grappling with my newly outed sexuality hadn't helped any.

Now that Dexter was getting to be older, she was slowly losing her grip on him. He was coming to me more and more, no matter what she tried to do to stop it. All she could do was sit back and pray that I didn't 'corrupt' our son like I had been.

I felt bad for her, I really did. Living in her mind must be hell.

"Kate."

"I'm not letting you change him, Xavier." She sounded out of breath. "It's not happening."

"I'm not going to do any of that. First of all, he's still a minor. And second, it's not my prerogative to force him into a lifestyle like that. He's my son, Kate. I love him just as much as you do. I would never ever do anything to jeopardize his autonomy like that."

Her sniffling on the other line broke my heart. As badly as our relationship had ended, I still cared for her. She was still the mother of my child and had been my wife. She hated me but that was all one sided.

I was mad at her for keeping Dexter from me, sure. Anyone would feel the same way. That didn't mean I wanted her to suffer like she clearly was. Whatever conspiracies were running through her mind were obviously ones she'd thought about for a long time.

Fear was her best friend, unfortunately.

"Why don't you think about it," I suggested. "I'm not planning on this trip for another week or two, anyway."

She didn't say anything back, just

continued to sniffle on the other end. Just as I was about to end the call, she said, "I'll talk to Dan."

All right, well at least that was one step in the right direction. "Okay. Just let me know. I'm planning the trip from Friday to Sunday. We'd fly back Sunday night."

"Do you have a flight already picked out?"

"Kind of. I have some that are available but I wanted to ask you first before I made anything solid."

"Oh," came her quiet response.

That was how it always went for us back in the day. I made the plans but she was the one with the final say. We worked that way, it gave her a sense of control that her upbringing never had. I'd recognized that early on—seen it in the way her parents treated her when we'd gone over for Sunday dinners.

It always made her happy in the end and was never any skin off my nose. Mostly because she usually agreed with me. Despite our differences, we, at one point, had made a pretty good team.

"All right. I'll let you know," she finally said.

"Thanks. You know how to reach me."

Ending the call, I let out a long sigh before running my hands over my face. I knew going into this it was going to be a monumental task, I just never accounted for how much it would take out of me in the end.

It would be worth it, though.

Dexter was worth it.

So long as Kate agreed to letting me have him for the weekend, we'd finally get that father-son bonding time that I'd been desperate for over the past fifteen years.

Hopefully, luck was on my side this time around.

CHAPTER SIX

Gage

"YOU REALLY THINK she's not going to let you take him?"

"I'm not sure." Xavier sounded exhausted on the other end of the line. "I'm hoping she does. That's all I can really do since she has full custody."

"I thought that shit didn't really matter once they turned sixteen? Can't they choose who to live with?"

Wasn't that how it worked?

Maybe I was being a dumbass in guessing. It wasn't like I ever had any experience with the system aside from CPS coming around that one time after my parents died.

"It's complicated. Dexter doesn't really know me so I don't exactly have a case."

Damn.

"He seems to be warming up to you, though."

"Barely," he mumbled. "But it's better than nothing."

"True."

I felt bad for Xavier. He was clearly trying. To no fault of his own, his son was being rather difficult. To a certain extent, I could understand the situation from both ends. Xavier had always wanted to be a father to Dexter but with his drinking, he'd made that pretty hard on the kid. So it wasn't exactly out of the blue that his kid was giving him the cold shoulder.

The past few months hadn't been as bad with Dexter agreeing to the occasional sit down dinner with Xavier. The sad thing was that it was nowhere near the level of closeness he wanted to have with his son.

On my end, I always felt guilty whenever Greyson and Asher were brought up in conversation. My brothers were close with me, even if sometimes they were little shits about it. When push came to shove, we were a family unit and nothing could break us apart. I'd been a whiny bastard with them leaving, but only out of sheer love for them.

Which is what made me hesitate in

bringing anything up to Xavier about them. I didn't want to rub it in my boyfriend's face that I had a relationship with the kids I'd raised while he didn't. Sure, his drinking and his highly erratic job hadn't done him any favors in that department—that didn't mean he had given up because he'd found his relationship with his son to be too hard to deal with.

"I told her to think about it," Xavier said. "So, now I just need to wait for her decision."

I wrinkled my nose at that.

From the stories I'd heard of Kate, I didn't like her. Sure, she'd been blindsided by Xavier's affair and had every right to divorce him and hate him for it. Taking it out on him using Dexter, though, was too low of a blow for me to forgive.

Why involve your child like that?

Why deprive him of a father, just because you didn't approve that he was gay?

That was the part that never made any sense to me, no matter what Xavier did to try and defend her actions. Or rather, seek some understanding with them.

I could get behind her not knowing how to navigate a co-parenting relationship with her ex after splitting with him, or even navigating the unknown about her ex being secretly gay and having to still be attached to him because of your shared kid. But the second she'd completely cut Xavier out of the equation and refused to work with him on visitation, that's where all sympathy for her was lost for me.

Trusting a woman like that who could so easily turn your child against you made a pit form in my stomach. If I were to ever run into her and meet her face to face... I really don't know what I'd do.

I'd be lucky not to spit some nasty shit at her.

"Well, I hope it works out."

"Gage."

Wincing, I realized that my tone had turned rather flippant. Sure, I was being kind of a bitch about the whole situation but fucking sue me. I missed my boyfriend. I wanted him here with me, even if it was only for a weekend and even if I had to keep my hands to myself until his son went to bed.

Having some ex-wife get in the way of all of that was making me fucking cranky.

"Sorry."

He chuckled softly. "I'm eager to see you, too. Don't worry."

"Okay, then hurry up and make her decide..."

"Oh, stop." I could hear the smile in his voice. "If this doesn't work out, that just means you need to come visit me."

"Hey, I can get behind that."

He laughed again. "Then it's settled. Either way, we'll be seeing each other soon."

I wanted to be happy about that... I really did.

These every few months of visiting were slowly starting to become not enough. Don't get me wrong, I loved every second I got to spend with Xavier, there was no doubt about that.

The problem laid in this: I wanted *more.* I was a greedy asshole who was getting tired of only receiving crumbs. When I'd agreed to a long distance relationship, I'd known that it was going to be difficult.

Everyone knew that, even if you weren't in one yourself. Out of hubris, I supposed I never considered how badly I'd be without Xavier. I had lived before him, so I figured I would be *fine* after him.

Clearly, I was dead fucking wrong.

"If the boys ever pity me and come back, I'll drag them along." Though, knowing them, they'd be questioning me the entire time while planning an elaborate prank.

Such is the way of two nineteen year olds.

"Maybe we can get them together with Dex."

"He needs new friends?" I teased.

"He needs friends in general."

Poor kid.

"As long as he can handle psychological warfare, then have at it."

"Think he's gotten enough of that growing up in the church, babe."

"True…" Though hopefully, it wasn't as bad as Xavier was predicting.

Apparently, Dexter had told him bits and pieces about getting dragged to church and put through intense religious indoctrination his entire life. And while I absolutely believed him, I hoped it also had no lasting effects.

Fuck knew that kid had been through enough already.

"I'm excited to see you," Xavier said, breaking me out of my thoughts.

I smiled and pressed the phone tighter to my ear. "I miss you. I hope we can see each other soon. I'm slowly dying over here."

"For my cock?"

Oh, that cheeky bastard. "More for that tongue of yours."

"Shit," he whispered.

"You at work?" I was already reaching for my crotch. My dick was already beginning to stiffen.

"Yes, so don't you dare start anything."

"Hey, I can't promise that I *won't* be sending you a dick pic after we end this phone call."

He swore again under his breath. "Gage. Behave."

"I'd love for you to make me."

"Oh, I will. The next time I get my hands on you."

Fuck, I loved the sound of that. "You got yourself a deal, Cruz."

CHAPTER SEVEN

Gage

APPARENTLY, PLANNING A Christmas party with a fire station full of rowdy adults was like trying to wrangle a bunch of goldfish into a net at the county fair— nearly fucking impossible.

As funny as it was to watch poor Ellie running around while trying to make sure everyone was signed up for at least *one* duty for the party, I also kind of felt bad for her. As our resident mother hen, she was probably the only one keeping us all from showing up with five raw turkeys, two side dishes and a hodge-podge of weirdly cut paper snowflakes tossed around.

"Wait, so who's in charge of the decorations now?" Jase rested his hands on his hips while he squinted at the bulletin board that was freshly tacked with the new list. "It can't just be me. There's no way I'm putting all that shit up by myself."

With Quinn snickering behind him and catching a stray slug to the arm, Jase turned to look over his shoulder at our party planner extraordinaire with his brow raised high.

"You've got Mark helping you out, too." Ellie had her usual clipboard in her hand, a pen tucked behind her ear to hold back a few stray pieces of hair while another one was in her hand ticking off something on the sheet in front of her. "I can throw Cyrus in there if you really need the extra manpower."

"Woah, woah." Hawke slapped his thighs while hiking himself up to his feet from where he'd been lounging against the steel bumper of one of the fire trucks. "We got dibs on the Scot. McWhiney over there can have someone else."

"You've got plenty of people on set up duty, dude," Jase argued.

"Dibs," Hawke repeated, a sly grin forming on his face.

Oh, if only Xavier were here to see all of this go down.

He'd be doubled over by now, laughing his ass off while ribbing me for having coworkers that loved to argue over a damn Christmas party. Having him here among the chaos would've been a nice change of pace, even if he'd have no fucking clue what was going on half the time.

I'd had plenty of good times with his coworkers off in Cali when I'd gone over for aerial training. Too bad he wouldn't get the same opportunity with mine.

"*Station Twenty-One,*" a voice over the intercom sounded off. "*Engine fifty-seven, respond to a multiple motor vehicle accident on Fifteen and Broad.*"

"Let's move!" Captain Clarke's voice boomed. "On-call, gear up! Standby, keep your walkies live!"

As I lifted myself up from where I'd settled down on the floor, the entire fire station came alive all in a flurry of calculated motion. Hustling over to my section to start passing out gear to the ones on duty today, my mind slipped into a straight-lined sense of focus, my hands busying themselves with unstrapping items from the wall in order to pass off to people.

This part of the job, while seemingly inconsequential, was one of the most important that a station had. Getting it wrong—such as gearing up a fellow coworker incorrectly—could be the difference between life and death in a dangerous situation.

Here, we took that shit seriously, no matter how much of a pain prep was at the ass crack of dawn.

Zander was the first one over to me after getting his coveralls on, Cyrus following close behind to the section next to me where Carmen was at. I tossed him a helmet, waiting for him to slip it on over his head and adjust it before handing off the rest of his gear and getting him suited up for the ride over.

He saluted me and jogged over to the fire truck, hopping up onto one of the metal rungs along with the rest of our on-call crew once they were geared up as well. The truck's engine rumbled to life, breathing a sense of excitement back into the otherwise quiet firehouse from just moments ago.

While this job had led to a lot of heartbreak in past times, the adrenaline rush was unmatched.

Things around here could change in an instant. From us arguing about party details, to moving into action, to potentially saving someone's life, all with the quick flip of a switch and our Captain at the helm of our well-oiled machine.

Our crew here were among the best and brightest in our entire state, and every damn time they were out in the field saving the people of our city, they made me fucking proud to be among them.

How could I not be when we were all a tight-knit family that kept each other safe in the face of danger?

Once the doors were lifted from the inside, the truck was navigated carefully out onto the street and soon disappeared, roaring off to whatever was waiting for them out there.

"Nice work, team," Captain Clarke said, the energy around us calming instantly as the garage was slowly pulled back down. "I'll keep an ear on the radio in case they call for backup."

The skeleton crew left behind all murmured our agreements before slowly dispersing back to our usual duties. With dispatch only calling for a single truck, that meant that whatever wreck our station was walking into was more than likely a minor fender-bender.

Per Louisiana law, though, we were required to be on scene on the off chance that something happened like a gas tank explosion or someone needing the Jaws of Life to get out of their totaled vehicle.

Other than that, hopefully it was going to be an easy day today.

"You still good for the potluck, Gage?" Ellie asked, making her way over to me.

"As long as you're good with me not cooking." The last thing anyone wanted me around was an oven. Or worse, a stove.

She squinted. With no clipboard in hand for her to tap her pen against, she resorted to using her hand for her nervous habit. "As long as it's still from that scratch kitchen you were talking about."

"Yup."

She breathed out a sigh of relief. "Okay, cool. Since you're all set, all I need to worry about is sorting out the knock-down crew."

"Let them fight over it," I suggested. "They'll figure it out."

She smiled in amusement. "I think you have too much faith in them if you believe they'll be able to bicker and come to an agreement."

"Hey, we need to let the kids figure it out for themselves once in a while."

That had her laughing which warmed

my heart. I hated seeing Ellie stressed, even if it was for something minor like a Christmas party.

"All right, true. Hey, you know, if you wanted to invite your man to come around for the get together, I'm sure everyone would be good with it."

"Wait, really?" Now, that was a little surprising. "You know he's in a different state, right?" I arched a brow at her.

Not to mention none of my coworkers had ever met the man before. It wasn't like we were going out to the bar and Xavier was tagging along. This would be an intimate get together with all of our families present.

Was that really the kind of thing that I could take a 'date' to?

Every year we did something for the holidays and every year, I went stag. It wasn't ever something that I'd cared about, mostly since for the past few years I'd had at least *someone* single to hang out with who wouldn't be tangled up in the romantic festivities.

Apparently, I'd missed thc mcmo, though, because this year, I'd be the only one left without a date. Besides, Ellie that is. She'd be running around making sure everyone was staying on their best behavior.

Ellie frowned. "You guys aren't going to see each other for Christmas? I know you're long distance, but that kind of sucks, if that's the case. He doesn't want to fly out or anything?"

Holding back from making a face was rather difficult.

We'd actually never had the discussion as of yet. Probably because I'd been avoiding the subject altogether ever since Xavier had brought up coming to see me with Dexter for his college tour soon.

Having him stay with me was already feeling like a 'too good to be true' scenario after our months long dry spell and jeopardizing that by getting down on my hands and knees and begging him to come to a Christmas party with me felt like asking too much of him.

Just because we'd been dating for almost an entire year didn't exactly give me the green light in having him fork over precious time he could be spending with his son before graduation hit. They'd only just started working out their issues with each other.

Guilting Xavier into spending time with me over the holidays because I was missing having my own family around felt kind of... well, wrong.

"Yeah... I'm not too sure about that," I said.

Ellie's frown deepened. "Tell me the boys are at least coming home?"

Ugh, another sore subject.

With still no word from either of them on what their plans were, I was left in total limbo. Hounding them for an answer was only going to make them dig their feet in—something I absolutely did *not* want to encourage.

I felt like we were already at a delicate state in our relationship, and given the fact that I was trying to tread lightly on the whole older brother/guardian thing while giving them the freedom in doing what they wanted now that they were fully grown adults, I already teetered on the 'overbearing' edge of the scale.

There were too many factors that could happen in me pushing them further away from me, even if unintentional. No matter what Xavier said, the multiple times he'd reassured me otherwise and that all of this was me simply getting caught up in my head and causing me to over think my brothers pulling away from me. My gut was telling me—or rather screaming at me—otherwise.

Trusting my instincts on this one was the best thing I could do. I had to be okay with the fact that they'd come back to me eventually, as all good things did once you set them free. A little bit of hands-off parenting wouldn't chase them away, no matter how crazy I felt inside of my own head over it.

At least, I hoped that was the damn case. I was kind of running around blind here.

How the hell did normal parents deal with this kind of shit on a daily basis?

Did it get easier with multiple kids?

It had to, right?

That's why people usually had a whole gaggle of them. By the time you got down to the fourth or fifth one, you were a pro at saying goodbye and the feeling of your heart absolutely being ripped out of your chest.

I felt a hand pat me on the shoulder, bringing me out of my thoughts. "You're doing that thing again."

"Shit, sorry, Ellie. The boys kind of have me wound up recently."

She smiled sympathetically. "My boyfriend has a kid who just turned sixteen and is in that wonderful rebellious phase. He says it gets easier."

"Wait, you've got a new man? Since when?" What the hell have *I* been missing?

She laughed. "It's a relatively recent thing, so relax. I'm planning on bringing him to the party. He'll need another newbie to bond with, so get your guy to come keep him company."

Sighing, I said, "I'll think about it."

Think being the keyword there.

She nudged an elbow into my ribs gently. "I really hope you do. Every time I see you on your phone, you light up. It'd be nice to finally meet the person keeping our Gage happy."

Damn.

Well, wasn't that the sweetest thing I'd ever heard.

"Thanks, Ellie."

She winked at me before sauntering off

to find her next victim, most likely in the form of Hawke, who'd she would hoodwink into letting her take Cyrus away and shoving him over into decorating for the party because of Jase's bitching.

Turning back to the bulletin board where all of our names were up on the duty sheet, I got lost in thinking. Maybe I really should try to invite Xavier to the Christmas party.

He'd probably say no and that was okay. Extending the offer was the least I could do, though. I would hate for him to find out after I let it slip that I had the opportunity to invite him and just didn't. If the situation were reversed, I'd feel hurt, too.

Besides, the worst he could tell me in the end was that he was planning on spending Christmas back home with Dexter.

Pulling my phone out of my vest and flipping it over, I noticed a text message already waiting for me. I'd missed the sound of the notification going off in the midst of the chaos in sending off my coworkers.

Opening it up, I saw Xavier's name at the top and his message directly underneath.

>>*Call me.*

CHAPTER EIGHT

Xavier

THE LAST THING I expected to wake up to that morning was a text from Kate's number telling me to call her with no other context given

While normally at that point I would've been pinching myself to make sure I wasn't in some sort of horrible nightmare where my ex was threatening to take my kid away from me again, my blaring alarm had those thoughts straightening right out and bringing me back down into reality.

Pulling myself out of bed while clutching my phone tight in my hand, I made my way into the kitchen to brew myself a cup of coffee that I'd most definitely need before I had any conversation with Kate.

While her text to me was simple in terms of her request, it also left my mind wandering far too much for my liking.

Obviously, the only reason she'd be contacting me was to discuss my upcoming trip with Dexter. And of course, judging by her text, I had absolutely no idea which way she was swaying toward.

The fact that she was even trying to contact me at all spoke to what little progress we'd made from the last time we'd talked. Sure, it wasn't much, but it was better than what we had before, which was complete stonewalling.

I'd take the stunted communication over that *any* day.

With my coffee finally brewed and a few sips down the hatch, I set my phone down on the counter after putting it on speaker and let the warmth from my mug seep into my hands to keep me steady.

Talking with Kate always set me on edge, no matter what the situation was. I wanted to lie to myself and pretend that I had no lasting effects from our divorce still lingering within me after running myself ragged going through therapy. However, the pounding of my heart told me otherwise.

Thankfully, she didn't keep me waiting too long, answering on the third ring.

"Hey."

"Morning," I said, hoping my pleasant tone was at least a little bit of a buffer for the inevitable awkwardness that was about to happen.

She didn't waste time on any of the pleasantries, cutting right to the chase. "I need to lay out some ground rules for this trip."

My heart fluttered in my chest. Jesus, she was actually going to let me take him. No trying to stonewall me into changing my mind or negotiating me down into keeping him here for a local trip. I was *actually* going to get to spend an entire weekend with my son and share an important experience with him—just the two of us.

I didn't know whether to thank Dan for talking some sense into her, or for Kate finally wanting to bury the hatchet for the time being. Either way, I was eternally grateful.

Clearing my throat, I said. "All right. Go ahead."

"He needs to call me every night before bed. I don't want any excuses that you guys got too busy and didn't have time. He's my son, too, Xavier. I want to hear from him. I see and talk to him every single day and this trip isn't going to keep me from that routine."

I could work with that. "Done."

She let out a soft sigh. "I also want updates on what you guys are doing. I... I may have went a little overboard in accusing you of wanting to take him to gay bars and stuff the last time we talked. I know... I know you wouldn't do anything to hurt him. I just—"

My mouth dropped open in disbelief while I stared down at my phone and her number lit up on the screen still.

Not only was that sounding a lot like an apology, but the fact that Kate was *recognizing* she'd fucked up in accusing me of doing something so heinous to our son was the exact last thing I ever expected to hear out of her mouth.

Maybe deep down, Kate really did want to trust me.

Her years of being resentful toward me made that nearly impossible—a situation of my own making, unfortunately—and while I never blamed her for hating me, I wished things could've been different.

If I was less of a coward in being honest with myself and those around me, if she and her family were less bigoted... So many possibilities of our futures having turned out differently could've happened.

Perhaps with this trip, I could show her that I wasn't out to get her or take our son away like she was so fearful of. All I wanted was to have some kind of relationship with him, much like she had this past decade without me in the picture.

I'd meant what I said when I'd told her about Dexter eventually spreading his wings and flying from the nest, leaving us far behind in his wake. The nature of kids was that was what eventually happened and as parents, we were supposed to come to terms with that on our own time.

Wanting to form some kind of bond with Dexter while he was still around was only natural. Especially, with him getting up there in age. He'd soon be moving from needing protective parents to needing us as guides while he began his own journey through life.

"How about I have him keep you updated every few hours," I suggested. "Sound fair?"

She was quiet for a while, eventually letting out another sigh. "Yes. That's fine."

"All right." This was all going so well that I had half a mind to ask her if I was being pranked. "Anything else?"

"Just... keep him safe. Please."

My heart softened at that. Deep down, Kate was just being a mom. Albeit, an overprotective one. But a mom, nonetheless. In her shoes, I'd be the same way. "Of course I will."

"Thank you." Her voice was quiet as she spoke.

"I'll book us plane tickets and send the

itinerary over to you once I've got it all sorted out."

"Okay. I'll be checking my email for it. And... Xavier?"

"Yes?"

"I hope you both have fun."

Smiling, I said, "Thanks, Kate. I hope so, too."

CHAPTER NINE

Xavier

THE FOLLOWING WEEK came and went in the blink of an eye and soon, our trip out to Baton Rouge was upon us.

Since telling Gage the good news right after my call with Kate, he'd been blowing up my phone with all of the local hot spots and attractions to take Dexter to after our tour of the campus. I found it all incredibly endearing how supportive he was about all of this, considering we probably wouldn't be seeing much of each other during most of the day.

I supposed it worked out in the end, considering the trip was a little on the short notice side of things and I hadn't given him enough of a head's up for him to be taking off time from the station. Still, he'd at least be home at a decent hour after work, which would give us plenty of down time to spend with each other after Dexter went to bed.

As much as I hated having to sneak behind my kid's back in order to spend time with my boyfriend, I'd take what I could get.

Waking Dexter up once we landed and were all clear to de-board, I grabbed our things from the carry-on overhead and ushered him down the aisle, sticking close to him as we left the plane.

"You sleep okay?" I asked.

His answering yawn was all the information I needed to know.

Chuckling, I led us down the loading bridge, dragging my suitcase behind me while keeping his duffle slung over my shoulder.

I was glad he'd slept on the plane. Getting to the airport bright and early this morning, while not exactly a struggle, had definitely been quite the trek for my kid. According to Kate, who'd been waiting outside with him when I'd pulled up, she'd caught him up in the middle of the night on his laptop, knee deep in some research that she hadn't been able to weasel out of him.

Fortunately, once we were safely tucked in my car and on the way to the airport, Dexter had shoved a hastily written itinerary at me with all of the sights he'd wanted to see while we were in Baton Rouge after our campus tour.

I'd gone over it on the plane, noting that most of them were ones that Gage had suggested, too. It made me happy that Dexter was looking forward to spending time with me, even if he didn't exactly know how to say it out loud.

These small moments that he was giving me were showing me that I wasn't the only one wanting to fix this. It was my job to, there was no question about that. Dexter meeting me halfway was nice, though.

Getting through the rest of the airport was easy enough. Since we didn't have any bags to check before leaving on our flight, we breezed through the rest of the terminals and made our way toward the main entrance.

"So..." Dexter said as we stepped onto the escalator that led down to the main part of the airport's lobby. "Your friend from training is picking us up... right?"

Turning to look at my son where he stood two steps above me, I nodded. "Yeah. I haven't gotten a chance to check my phone to let him know we're here. But he said he didn't live too far from here."

"Yeah... I don't know that you're going to need to do that."

Instantly, my brows were furrowing. "Why do you say that?"

If Dexter wasn't comfortable riding in a car with Gage back to his place, then we'd figure something else out. I fucking loathed rideshares with a burning passion, but if it made my kid more comfortable, then whatever.

Looking at him, though, he didn't *seem* put off by the idea. In fact, he was wearing a rather bemused expression, his gaze focused away from me as he looked over my head at something.

"I think he's already here."

Whipping around, my gaze darted to the couple in front of us, and then past them to where the main lobby had travelers coming and going. In the midst of the flurry of people, a lone man stood in the middle with a crudely decorated sign that was being held up, the words, *'Welcome to Baton Rouge!'* in scrolling font.

As soon as he spotted us—or rather *me*—he lifted the sign high above his head and waved it at us, that familiar, blinding grin practically splitting his face in half.

Oh, Gage.

"He always that peppy?" Dexter asked.

Snorting, I nudged my elbow backward into his side. Yep."

I paused at the bottom of the escalator while Dexter stepped off right behind me. He kept himself close to me as we made our way through the bustling crowds and over to where Gage stood.

He lowered his sign just in time to avoid a couple cutting between us, narrowly catching him in the shoulder and checking him backward. As weird as it was to be back in Baton Rouge after so many months of being gone, it was nice to know that the people out here were just as oblivious as they were back in Cali.

"Hey." Gage's arms came up from his sides, the knee-jerk reaction to reach out and hug me short circuiting at the last moment when his gaze darted to the side, catching sight of Dexter coming up next to me. He shifted fluidly into shoving his arm in my son's direction, holding out his hand. "Nice to meet you, Dexter. Your dad's told me a lot about you."

Politely, my son took Gage's hand and shook it, throwing me an eyebrow raise while saying, "Really?"

"Yup." Gage flashed him another blinding smile. "All good things. Don't worry."

Dexter dropped his hand back to his side, narrowing his eyes curiously while his gaze flitted between us.

Fuck, I hoped we weren't being obvious with all of this. The last thing I needed Dexter to pick up on was our god awful budding sexual tension that literally never seemed to go away no matter what we did.

Thankfully, Gage was always the master of distraction and cleared his throat to ask, "Flight go okay?"

"Yeah. No turbulence." Readjusting Dexter's bag on my shoulder, I nodded toward the entrance of the airport. "How is it out there?"

Gage laughed. "Oh, you're going to hate it."

Damn it...

"Why?" Dexter asked. "We're used to the heat in the winter time."

"Humidity's a bitch here, kid," I said, nudging him. "We're in swamp territory."

"Hey! It's not as bad as the summer," Gage argued. "It's only seventy percent right now."

Dexter's mouth dropped open while I let out a soft curse under my breath. See, this was the thing about coming down to the south. While the heat wasn't bad, it was the humidity that made it feel like you were walking through a damn sauna.

I could deal with hundred-degree heat and no humidity. But put me in the mid-seventies with a humidity of eighty percent? I was fucking done for.

"Ew..." Dexter muttered.

"See? I'm not the only one," I said.

Gage folded up his sign and waved it at both of us. "Come on, you two complainers. I've got the AC running in the car. Valet's holding it for me right outside."

Now, that's what I was talking about.

I fought the urge to reach over and slap Gage's ass when he turned and walked in front of us. All right, maybe this whole 'keeping our hands to ourselves' thing was going to be a lot harder than I imagined.

CHAPTER TEN

Gage

"MAKE YOURSELVES AT home. Whatever you need, let me know," I said, swinging the door closed behind me.

My house wasn't large by any means—comfy enough to house three people and not feel like we were all on top of each other. I'd already made the bed up in Asher's room, leaving the one next to mine, Greyson's, empty. Lord knew if we'd need it once Dexter went to bed and Xavier finally got his hands on me.

He probably thought he was being slick with those subtle looks of his that he'd been throwing my way in the car whenever I glanced over at him at a red light. Or the way his hand twitched on his thigh while he was fighting the urge to grab onto mine whenever I switched the gearshift.

Xavier was funny that way—always trying to hold himself back on account of trying to maintain that carefully crafted facade of calm he favored around other people. The most ironic part about all of that—or was it the most beautiful?—was how completely undone he became when we got together.

The way his jaw would go slack just as he was about to come, or how tense his body got while driving himself into me, getting those long strokes inside of me as deep as possible. God, everything about us having sex drove me fucking wild and had my toes curling inside of my shoes.

"Earth to Gage." Hearing my name being called broke me out of my dirty thoughts instantly.

Putting on a pleasant smile, I waved my hand toward the living room and showed my guests inside. "Here is the rest of the house. Bedrooms are down on the left with fresh sheets tucked nice and neat. Kitchen's on the right and the fridge *is* freshly stocked. Bathroom is across from the master and has new towels on the sink up for grabs."

Xavier's lip twitched. "You didn't need to do all of that, you know."

Winking, I said, "Let me pamper, okay?

This house is in need of guests."

While Xavier breathed out a laugh, Dexter's gaze wandered around the living room. I hoped he'd find himself comfortable here. Seeing as I was kind of dating his dad pretty seriously, and hoped to for a long time, this little trial visit was a bit make or break.

"You like video games?" I offered, nodding for him to follow me into the living room where I had the entertainment set up.

He was hesitant to follow, but did so after a nod from his dad who soon disappeared down the hall with their bags.

"Uh... yeah. Kind of."

Grinning, I pulled open the door to all of Asher and Greyson's consoles to show him. "My brothers are closet nerds. While they're away, feel free to use whatever. It's all already hooked up to the Smart system."

He blinked in surprise. "Where are your brothers?"

That had me blowing out a breath, more out of frustration than anything. "They're west and east of here, ignoring me. One's in Texas, the other's over in Georgia."

"Oh," was all Dexter said to that.

Quiet kid.

I remembered how Xavier had said he was worried about his kid's social life not too long ago. Maybe sometime in the future, if all went well this weekend and I didn't scare Dexter off completely, he'd warm up to meeting the boys.

Now *that* would be the true testament to how much chaos Dexter could handle.

"You off from school for long?" I asked, swinging the entertainment unit door shut. "I haven't kept up with school schedules in a while since my brothers graduated."

"I've got winter break coming up. I already finished my end of semester tests so my mom let me come on this trip with my dad."

I wondered how true that really was. Not that I doubted Dexter's sincerity or anything, I just didn't foresee Xavier's ex-wife being so... charitable with letting her son go away with his dad for an entire weekend. I'm obviously biased here, sue me. The stories from Xavier about her, though, still got my blood boiling.

"Well, hopefully you like LSU," I said, plastering on a smile again. "The campus is really nice. I pass it on the way to work every day."

"My dad said you're a firefighter."

"Guilty."

"So... that's how you two met, right?"

For some reason, the way he was asking almost sounded like he was fishing for something. Fuck me, I should've gotten the full story from Xavier on what he'd told his kid regarding us. All I knew was that he was playing our relationship on the down low to keep Dexter from getting uncomfortable.

Which... sucked.

At the same time, it wasn't like either Xavier or I could help that he was raised in a strictly religious household and had no idea what kind of beliefs he had. He knew his dad was out and gay, so at least we weren't going to be running into any problems regarding *that* topic.

Me on the other hand?

I had no idea what the hell I was supposed to be playing this as.

Friend?

Former coworker?

All of them sounded like nails on a chalkboard to me.

Sometimes even *boyfriend* did that, too, but what else was I supposed to call Xavier?

Lover sounded like too much and partner made it confusing when half of us at the station referred to each other that way when working.

"Actually, I went to California to train under him for an aerial program and brought back a lot of what I learned to my station," I said, rubbing my hands together a few times. "I can practically fly fighter jets now." I let out a chuckle and flashed him a grin.

To my utter surprise, Dexter let out a small snort.

All right, progress.

"We doing okay out here?" Xavier poked his head around the corner, both of his brows pulled together in that nervous way of his.

Just as I was about to give him the big old thumbs up, the sound of my radio flagging from where I had it on the charging dock by the door filtered around the room.

Of all fucking times…

"Damn," I mumbled. "Well, duty calls."

"Be safe." Xavier flashed me a smile, his hand flexing into a fist at his side, clearly fighting himself from grabbing at me like he would've any other time.

In response, I clenched my teeth

together. Man, I wanted to close the distance between us and peck him on the way out—and judging by his pinched expression, he wanted that, too.

Behave. It's only for a few more hours.

"Have fun today!" I said, and jogged to my bedroom to grab my uniform before heading out.

Never in my life had I ever prayed for some crazy situation to be thrust into when I got to the station, not wanting the bad luck and karma to follow me to my next life.

Today was my exception. Because damn right I was going need all of the distractions in the world that I could possibly get to keep me from jumping Xavier's bones the second I laid my eyes on him again.

That man was temptation on two legs

and I was the stupid moth entranced by his flame.

CHAPTER ELEVEN

Xavier

"YOUR FRIEND SEEMS..."

Inwardly, I winced, waiting for Dexter to finish his sentence and tell me he absolutely hated Gage. That would be my luck, honestly, after finally finding a boyfriend I clicked with so damn well that I could've sworn the man was my soul mate.

In an ironic sense, I deserved

something like that coming my way for absolutely fucking up Dexter's life with my alcoholism and breaking his mother's heart, among the thousand other things I'd done to hurt others in my past. Those were just my two biggest transgressions at the moment.

I was sure if I thought about it longer than a few seconds, I'd find more I needed to *repent for,* or whatever it was that Kate's parents had spat out at me after finding out I was gay.

"Actually. He kind of surprised me," Dexter finally said.

I glanced over at him as we walked down the street, heading toward a cafe from his itinerary that he was interested in visiting. Apparently, it was one of those fancy cat cafes that allowed you rent a table while cats came and went during your stay.

Funny, I'd never considered my son to be a cat person—seeing as how his mother was deathly allergic—but the more I was getting to know him, the clearer I was beginning to see it. There was so much to Dexter that I just *didn't know* and my desperate need to figure him out was blinding.

"Really?" I asked. "What makes you say that?"

He shrugged at me, shoving both of his hands into his pockets. "I don't know. He's really nice. And accommodating."

"What, you don't think I can be friends with nice people?"

He rolled his eyes at me. Such a teenager. "That's not what I meant."

"Tell me, then." *Because I'm seriously dying to know.*

He shrugged again. "I don't know. I guess... I kind of pictured you being friends with a bunch of meatheads."

Huffing out a laugh, I grabbed onto the door to the cafe when we approached it and nodded for him to duck under my arm and head inside. "The only true meathead I know is currently engaged to an ex-felon."

And what a fucking phone call *that* was to receive on a Friday night after coming back from one of my AA meetings.

Did I expect anything less from Jackson fucking Hall to have fallen in love with someone with a rap sheet?

Not exactly. Getting it out of him on *how* he met this man was actually the more wild part of the story that I still couldn't exactly wrap my head around.

But whatever.

Love was love, right?

"What?" Dexter gave me a bewildered look.

I shook my head, grabbing him lightly by the shoulder in order to steer him toward the register. "It's a long story. Point is, I've got friends in all sorts of varieties."

"I see that," he mumbled at me.

After paying for drinks and two small pastries, we grabbed a small floor table and settled down comfortably.

The cafe turned out to be really nice and clean considering they had about thirty cats roaming around. Some sat on perches nailed to the walls above our heads, some wandered the floor looking for handouts, and some, like the two that were currently occupying *our* table, were just plain old cuddle bugs looking for attention.

I sipped my coffee silently while watching Dexter's rare smile grace his face, one of his hands buried in the long fur of a pretty white cat and his other stroking over the head of an orange tabby that had completely commandeered his lap the moment we sat down.

Seeing my son happy was a nice change of pace from our usual standoffs. I liked seeing this side of him, even if it was only for the small window he'd let me in today.

"Too bad we can't take one home," he said after a while.

"I know. You could always come back here and adopt one if you decide to go to LSU."

His mouth thinned into a straight line. "Yeah... maybe."

"You thinking about going somewhere else?"

Dexter sighed. "I don't know. Mom's going to kill me either way, so..."

Setting down my mug slowly gave me the time to reel back my sudden shock of anger and the snap back reaction I would normally have come up with. The protectiveness I felt for him regarding his mother was always going to be there, no matter what I did or how much time passed. My therapist had been pretty straightforward in telling me that it was a trauma response from Dexter being ripped away from me as he had been and my having no say in the matter afterward.

Here was the thing, though—I didn't *want* to still hold onto this resentment. It ate away at me little by little each time it flared up. Just like my PTSD did from my military days. Letting it go was my goal, and damn was it hard to do anytime something like this reared its ugly head.

Whatever Kate's reasons are, they make sense to her.

Even if sometimes I felt like she was being way too fucking paranoid.

"Why do you say that, Dex?"

"Because she's expecting me to go to the local community college. Apparently, Dan's got some in with the Dean or whatever and they can get me in without having me take an admissions test."

Not to turn my nose up at a community college or anything but that seemed like a rather strange solution, seeing as how Dexter was clearly smart enough—and had the grades—to get into a state school. On top of that, it was a school not even in our home state.

That said a lot about his academic prowess.

"Hm." Drumming my fingers on the table, I focused my attention on the cat in his lap who was happily licking at his hand. "You tell her about applying elsewhere?"

He shook his head. "Like I said, she'd freak out. She doesn't even want me staying in a dorm."

"*Why?*"

Dexter glanced up at me, his lips parting to say something just as one of the bus boys was coming around with a small bucket tucked under his arm to collect the stray dishes left by other customers. When he reached our table, he glanced down at the two cats in Dexter's lap and grinned widely.

"You got the best ones in the house."

He squatted down to our table so he wasn't hovering above us. His long wavy hair fell across his shoulder when he reached out to offer his hand to the white cat. "They're a bonded pair, but you probably guessed that already."

Dexter stared at him with slightly wide eyes. They were around the same age, if I had to take a stab in the dark. Unlike my son, though, this boy had a lip hoop punched into either side of his mouth and wore a few bangles around his wrist that clanged together when he teased the cat with his fingers.

He was a handsome kid, if not a little gangly for a teenager. A soft laugh escaped him when the white cat turned to rub up against his hand comfortably.

"His name's Fritz," he said, not talking to me at all. "The one in your lap is

Steve."

"O-oh," was all Dexter stuttered out.

"They're both up for adoption. But I do have to warn you, they have to go together."

Dexter merely nodded mutely in response, his cheeks slightly colored in a soft shade of red.

Oh.

I think... I was beginning to see why Kate was digging her nails so hard into our kid. Why she was so damn adamant on keeping a watchful eye on both Dexter and I while we were off on this trip. Maybe it wasn't some kind of motherly paranoia after all, but something else entirely.

The bus boy finally lifted himself back up to his feet, bidding us a farewell while throwing a wink at Dexter that had my son quickly averting his eyes and focusing back down at the cat in his lap.

Leaning over slowly, I let both of my arms rest on top of the table while I wrestled with reaching over and grabbing at him to get him to look at me. I settled on giving him space instead because he clearly needed it. "Dex. You... know you can tell me anything, right? I won't ever judge you."

God, I hoped he knew that.

There was nothing in this world that would ever make me love him less. Especially... something like this. Feelings were so damn complicated and as a teenager trying to figure out your place in the world, that made it all the more harder to come to terms with being different than everyone else around you.

Especially, in an evangelical household.

XAVIER

His Adam's apple visibly bobbed as he swallowed. "Yeah. Sure. Whatever. Can we go?"

CHAPTER TWELVE

Xavier

WE SPENT THE rest of the morning into late afternoon in relative silence, wandering the small section of the city Dexter had chosen for the day.

I didn't want to push him into talking to me about anything when he was clearly very uncomfortable in doing so. For whatever reason, he wasn't able to trust me just yet with letting me in. He needed time to figure it out, something I could absolutely sympathize with.

I had no idea if my hypothesis was even correct in assuming he'd found that bus boy attractive. Hell, I could be way off base in assuming that, and for all I knew, he'd just never really met another guy his age with lip piercings, long hair, and a healthy appreciation for cats.

I was sure Kate was keeping his circle small in order to fit in with her church-going friends and family, and it would be no surprise to me given that, to my knowledge, Dexter didn't have the biggest group of friends at school to begin with.

He was a quiet kid. Kept his head down most of the time and worked his ass off to get where he was with his grades. I mean, clearly, considering LSU wanted to give him a full ride and everything.

XAVIER

My kid was smart enough to go and do whatever he wanted. My only hope was that he wasn't held back by the need to keep his mom happy.

Getting back to Gage's place, we were greeted by the smell of something cooking from the kitchen. After walking for so long under the blazing southern sun, I was ready to chow down on whatever was placed down in front of me.

Leaving Dexter to take off his shoes in peace, I wandered my way into the kitchen, spotting Gage bent over a large boiling pot. He was still in his uniform, though much more wrinkled than how he'd left in it this morning.

Glancing back over my shoulder to make sure I didn't have a straggler following after me, I came up behind him and wrapped my arms around his waist.

He sagged into me instantly, tilting his head back to give me access to his neck to leave a trail of kisses up to his ear.

"Missed you," he sighed softly.

I did, too. Badly.

I breathed him in, dreading having to let him go in a few seconds. He felt perfect nestled back against my chest, his body weight a solid form that I could grab onto versus the figment I'd imagined when we were on the phone every night.

This was what I wanted to come home to every night. Not my empty house with just the sad white walls to keep me company.

"How was your tour around the city?" he asked, looking back at me when I finally forced myself to let go of him.

"Fine. Went to a few places." Nodding to the pot, I asked, "What's all that?"

"No clue. I'll be honest, I totally picked it up from the grocery store on the way home. The package told me to add water and voila."

God, he was so damn charming.

I laughed, swiping the ripped open container off of the counter. "Seafood boil, huh..."

"Southern classic."

My hands itched to grab onto him again and wrap him up into a tight hug while we listened to the sounds of the pot boil in the background. That kind of domestic shit was something I never thought I'd want. I'd been too hardened by my days in the military to settle down into a life of seafood boils and relaxed conversations after a long day at work.

At least, that's what I'd believed. Now I knew deep down, I'd always craved that kind of connection. I'd searched for it for years in between hook-ups and dating stints that never seemed to work out in my favor.

No one could handle my brand of fucked up, that's what I'd believed. Right up until I met Gage and he'd flipped my world completely upside down.

Leaning over, I stole another kiss before backing off completely. "Work went okay?"

"Yeah, had a small house fire but we got it down before it spread to the neighbors. Not much damage other than the family room in the back."

"Electrical failure?" I guessed.

"Worse. Cat knocked over a candle and set the carpet on fire. The house hadn't had an update since the seventies, so you can only imagine how crispy that carpet was when it went up.”

Damn, that sucked. “Least it was only a portion of the house.”

“What’s what our Captain said. Insurance should pay it out, and hopefully, get them a whole new renovation.”

“What happened?” Dexter asked, wandering into the kitchen. His gaze immediately zeroed in on the pot on the stove.

“Oh, just talking shop.” Gage waved his wooden spoon in the air. “You like seafood, Dexter?”

“Never really had it.”

Gage gasped obnoxiously and then had the audacity to pin a glare in my direction. “What the hell are you feeding this poor boy? Scraps?”

Out of the corner of my eye, I watched

the bemused smile cross over my kid's face.

"Funny," I said, bringing my hand up to smack his ass but diverting in time in order to slap his shoulder instead. "Says the man who got it store bought."

"Look, you either want it homemade or edible. You can't have both in this house," he argued.

"Your poor brothers," I teased.

He leveled me with the end of his wooden spoon. "They were fed. That's all that matters."

"According to who?"

He threw a wink at me. "CPS."

Shaking my head and turning back to Dexter, I said, "We can find you something else to eat if you want. I'm sure Gage won't cry himself to sleep for too long tonight."

To my surprise, Dexter's smile widened an inch. "I'll try it. As long as it's edible."

Gage held a hand to his chest in a mock salute. "Scouts honor."

As Gage turned back to the stove to stir his pot, I shuffled both Dexter and I out of the kitchen to give the man some peace and quiet while he finished up. "I don't know about you, but I'm ready to get out of these sticky clothes. Louisiana humidity is no joke."

I didn't know how the hell Gage was able to function in this weather. California residents got a bad wrap for being babies in the wintertime when our temps dipped below sixty-five, but holy hell was the swamp miserable.

Dexter followed me, nodding along. I slipped my shirt off of my body, instantly feeling relief from no longer having the damn material clinging to me.

"Hey, dad?"

I whipped my head around. "Yeah."

Dexter drummed his fingers along the doorframe to his room in a rhythm that sounded familiar but I couldn't quite put my finger on where it was from. He searched my expression for something, finally settling with a nod as he spoke again. "He's a good man."

My eyes widened.

And with that, he disappeared beyond the door to get changed.

CHAPTER THIRTEEN

Xavier

HE'S A GOOD man.

There had only been two other times my heart had ever felt so full—the day Dexter was born and the day we got to bring him home from the hospital.

He's a good man.

God, he really fucking was, wasn't he?

Sticking by me through my journey to sobriety. Helping me into it in the first place. Hell, *pushing* me to be a better man when it came to my kid and repairing the damage from my past with him. Coming to terms with my PTSD and what happened during my military career.

Gage was a one of a kind gem that I honestly never deserved to have, let alone keep all for myself. He deserved someone way less fucked up than me and yet, he'd told me plenty of times that he wouldn't have it any other way.

He got along with my kid, despite his standoffish nature. Made him *laugh.*

How the hell did I earn a man like Gage?

Rolling out of bed and kicking off my covers, I slapped my hand on the nightstand next to the bed until I felt the familiar shape of my phone. Lifting it up, I sent off a quick text to Gage to see if he was still up.

When the response came a minute later, beckoning me to his room, all I felt was the giddiness of a love sick teenager sneaking out late to meet up with my boyfriend.

Thankfully, the house was quiet when I opened the door to my room.

Across the way, Dexter's door remained closed with him, hopefully, already asleep inside. While we'd turned in a little early after dinner, I figured that given our traveling this morning and our hike around the city, all of it would've tuckered him out in no time.

Gage's door was already cracked from the jam, allowing me to slip inside and close it behind me without making a single sound. He was sitting up in bed waiting for me, his hair still damp from a shower, the lamp on his nightstand dimmed to give the room that perfectly romantic ambiance he was constantly joking with me about over the phone.

I went to him quickly, lifting him up from the bed at the same time as he reached for me to wrap his arms around my waist. Our lips crashed into each other, both of us hungry for a taste of what we'd been dying to have over the past few months.

A small moan rumbled up his throat, quickly cut short when I tilted him backward onto the bed and laid him flat on his back. Our hips ground into each other almost of their own accord once I was on top of him, one of Gage's legs coming up to hook around my left side.

Ripping my lips away from his, I grabbed at his jaw. "I might have to gag you."

I loved how loud Gage got but scarring my poor kid with the sounds of his dad pounding ass was the *last* thing I wanted.

"Fuck," he whimpered.

"Think you can behave for me?" I licked a line down from his lips to his chin where stubble was starting to come in. It prickled my skin, sending a shiver racing down my spine.

"No."

Well, at least he was being honest.

Leaning back, I searched Gage's room for anything that I could use to stuff into his mouth for the time being. There were only a few more precious minutes I had left with all of my brain cells before I devolved into that of a caveman.

Under me, Gage rolled his hips into mine again, causing us both to gasp.

He was such a shit when he was horny.

Before he could utter another sound, my hand quickly slapped over his mouth, muffling it. "You're killing me."

His eyes twinkled in the dim light.

Looking down at him, I noted he was barely wearing anything. Just a simple cotton t-shirt and a pair of loose boxers that were doing absolutely nothing to hide how aroused he was. Honestly, I wasn't much better off in my sleep shorts, the front of which was jutting out from my hips.

Taking my hand off of his mouth and untangling his leg from around me, I slipped myself off of the bed and grabbed a hold of hips, using them to help me flip him over onto his stomach. Gage was already propping his ass up for me by the time I had my t-shirt stripped off and my sleep shorts tossed onto the floor.

"Head in the mattress, baby." Using both of my hands, I grabbed onto the ass that had been teasing me since damn near bright and early this morning, both cheeks fitting in my palms perfectly while I squeezed them a few times.

Perfect.

So goddamn perfect.

Gage's back arched beautifully, leading me to have to bite down on my tongue hard enough to hurt in order to hold back a moan teasing at the back of my throat. Letting go of his ass, I quickly slipped his boxers down his thighs.

He kicked them off one leg at a time, slipping his body forward on the mattress until his upper half was flush with it while he kept his lower half propped up for me. He was such a fucking sight to see, tempting me into wanting to take a picture for my private folder for when I was back home and lonely with only my hand to keep me company.

"Drawer," he said, lifting a finger to point at the one next to his bed.

Leaning over to it, one hand already fisted around the base of my cock, I tugged it open. A single bottle of lube was inside, haphazardly thrown from the last time he'd used it the night before my flight over here when I'd told him to send me a picture of his fingers in his ass for me.

"You're so good at reading me," I said, grabbing the bottle and shoving the drawer closed.

"Xavier, I need you so fucking bad." He whimpered again.

"I know, baby. One more second, I promise."

He was being so patient, letting me get a good look at him before I gave him even a modicum of relief with my touch. Snapping the cap open on the lube, I drizzled a good amount down my cock before tossing it onto the bed.

While working it over myself, I leaned in and planted my mouth right over his hole, delighting in the muffled squeal as Gage buried his head back into the mattress again. I swirled my tongue around his puckered opening, teasing him with the tip before retreating to lap up at his rim again.

His hips gyrated back against my mouth, trying to get as much friction as possible. My hand ached to slap at his ass cheek, to give him a little pain with his pleasure just as he liked. The problem was that my slaps were never quiet and clapping him good and loud on the ass was the only way to do it.

I wasn't into those love taps. A handprint needed to be left behind to appreciate in all its rosy pink glory for it to actually have been worth it.

Before I let myself get too carried away with my thoughts, I popped my mouth off of him and gave him a quick nip, then leaned back. I propped my leg up on the edge of his bed frame, tucking my foot between it and the mattress on top to keep me steady while I caught his hip with my free hand to hold him still.

He groaned at that, already anticipating me sliding into him.

"You've been keeping yourself nice and ready for me, right?" I asked, already knowing the answer but needing to hear it from his mouth anyway.

He tilted his head to the side, mumbling out a tangled 'yes' that was mixed with a quiet moan.

"Good," I praised, sliding the tip of my cock around his hole to coat him generously. His hole was already fluttering, desperately trying to catch my cock with every pass over his pucker.

Finally, I pressed against him, letting myself dip into his hot center slowly. Apparently, Gage was a little less patient than I'd given him credit for and all but slammed himself back against me.

"Fuck..." came my hissed curse, as I nearly erupted right then and there.

This man is truly going to be the death of me.

My balls ached with the need to just let

it all go and flood his insides, throwing all of our careful prep right out the window like we were a couple of virgins on our wedding night. My fingers tight on his hip, I held him in place until I could calm down enough not to actually come the second I moved again.

Which I'm sure he'd love to brag about. Bastard.

Blowing out a long breath, I rolled my hips back until only the head of my cock was seated inside of him. Then, I slammed forward, pulling him back onto me in the same singular motion that had me burying myself as deep as I could go.

His body jolted, both of his hands fisting in the sheets while he kept his face down against the mattress. I rocked my hips again, mimicking the motion from before as his tight heat gripped me perfectly, squeezing when I bottomed out, my hips pressed tightly against the globes of his ass.

This was what was perfect about Gage. His body was so attuned to me that it knew exactly what I needed.

One of his hands untangled from the sheets, coming around to reach between his legs. I slapped his hand away, grabbing onto his cock with my own.

"Mine."

No way was he coming before I told him he could.

He tried to rock back against me, not getting very far when I dug my fingers into his hips again, my nails leaving crescent shaped red marks in his skin. He was trapped in my rhythm game, completely at my mercy just like we'd both been fantasizing about for the past few weeks.

"You missed me filling you like this, baby, didn't you," I whispered, moving my hand down to cup his balls and squeeze them.

He choked out a moan, grabbing onto the sheets again out of desperation.

"That's it." A small grunt worked its way up my throat. "You're... mmmm, so fucking tight."

Fuck, I was *not* going to last.

I'd been without him too long. I wasn't used to how fucking incredible he felt wrapped around me like this. I could only get myself off so much, my hand paling in comparison to the real deal.

Moving back up to fist Gage's cock once again, I stroked him in time with my thrusts as I pounded my hips against his ass. His body braced against the bed, taking each thrust with his unmoving form.

"Oh fuck," came tumbling out of my mouth, just as the first spurts of cum shot out of him and drizzled all over my fingers.

I followed closely behind, slamming into him one more time before stiffening and letting myself come inside of his tight heat. Both of us collapsed onto the bed, toppled over in a damn tangled pile of limbs that I knew we were going to wake up sore from in the morning.

Neither of us cared, too busy catching our breath and letting the post-orgasm haze settle over us. With my hand still wrapped around his cock, I pressed soft kisses along his shoulder and neck before burying my face there.

He let out a content sigh, relaxing under me.

"Love you," was all I could mumble before letting my eyes slide closed.

CHAPTER FOURTEEN

Xavier

LSU'S CAMPUS WAS huge.

With a sprawling greenery that was the size of a small town, surrounded by dozens of buildings that made up the rest of the property, it made it easy to get lost once you were past the front entrance gates.

There were a couple of signs here and there pointing toward different directions, but outside of that, you were on your own.

Dexter and I had left early this morning and grabbed a bite to eat before coming over here, giving us the time to wake up and recharge before we took on the massive undertaking of exploring this entire place before we were due back to Gage's house for lunch at one.

With it being winter break, almost the entire campus was deserted aside from us wandering around. Which was kind of nice. Not many people got this kind of an unfettered tour of a potential school without being hassled by a second year tour guide trying to upsell you on the meal package.

As much as it'd kill me to have Dexter living so far away from me, I could see him walking across these soon-to-be-busy sidewalks getting to class with his backpack stuffed to the brim with textbooks and notes. I could see him proudly repping the purple and yellow colors of LSU and excitedly telling anyone who asked him where he was going for his four-year degree.

All of this could be the dad in me being proud of my kid even before he actually agreed on committing to a college before we could even tour one fully. I never had any doubts in me that he'd get into a great school, regardless. He had the drive to go far in life in whatever he wanted to do. Anyone could see that.

"They've got a huge sports program here," Dexter told me while passing by the gates heading toward the stadium. From here, I could spot the familiar yellow goal posts rising up over the buildings blocking the field from view. "They've put a lot of money into their football team."

I raised my brow. "You interested in something like that?"

His head snapped to me while a small snort escaped him. "No offense, dad, but do I look like the type to do a sports program?"

Ironically, he had my build, just without all of the muscle attached to it. He was still a growing kid, though, young enough that his second bout of puberty hadn't yet hit. So, there was still time.

Mentally, though?

No, I couldn't see Dexter running around a football field and getting slammed to the ground while trying to wrestle around for a pigskin.

"Hey, I'm not here to judge your interests," I teased.

If anything, I wanted to encourage whatever it was he typically occupied his time with. Reading, exercising, lounging around playing video games. None of that mattered to me as long as he was happy and still kept up his grades.

Back in the day with my own dad, I'd never had the luxury of sitting around doing nothing. He was of the old school mindset that moving equaled productivity and relaxing was born out of laziness. I'd had a lot of pent up energy when I was younger, which translated to keeping myself busy whenever I had any kind of downtime.

Hence the military.

After a while, though, it weighed on me. I'd had a hard time transitioning into civilian life—my whole adolescence having been molded into creating anxiety anytime I didn't at least keep my hands busy. Sometimes, I wondered if that was the reason I'd ever picked up the bottle in the first place.

Alcohol quieted my racing mind like no other. Once my PTSD took control, abusing it was just another step on my already growing totem pole of vices that would eventually kill me one day.

These days, forcing myself to relax was like learning an entirely new language. I was clunky at it, bad at practicing when I should be, and had a habit of wanting to rely on my old ways in order to make myself feel better.

My therapist had said that, as a form of perfectionism, trying once and failing had resulted in me giving up. Hearing that for the first time spun me around for days. I'd never considered myself to *be* a perfectionist. And yet the more internal work I'd done, and the more I uncovered who I *really* was, the more accurate that damn statement was.

Haunting me, to this day.

I'm proud that I never went back to the bottle. It'd been tempting as all hell, don't get me wrong. Falling back into my old habits, as my therapist had said, would be taking the easy way out. But I'd be damned if I became a quitter.

I hadn't been raised that way and I certainly wasn't going to start.

Dexter nudged me with his elbow, reaching for the door to the main academic building and holding it open for me. "Football's not really my cup of tea."

"So what is?" I asked, stepping inside and waiting for him to follow me before we began strolling leisurely down the long hallway.

The place was three stories, large glass panes stretched up to the ceiling that had round tables on the other side of it, facing out toward the main lobby. The staircase leading up to the first floor was more grand than I'd ever seen a college have.

Twin banners were hanging from the ceiling over the staircase in that familiar purple.

Down on the main floor were a couple of tables with the chairs put up on top of them. A lone janitor was buffing out a part of the floor a few feet away from us with headphones covering his ears. He barely glanced up at us as we walked toward the stairs and took them up to the next level.

"I know it's going to sound lame, but I actually do like to study," he said, clutching the railing as we stepped. "I like learning. A lot of people think that's a nerdy thing to say, but it's genuinely true."

"Nothing wrong with that, kid. We need more booksmart people in this world."

He blew out a breath. "Yeah, I guess. It kind of makes me feel like an outcast, though. People my age care about social media and followers. That sort of thing. There's nothing wrong with that, I just don't... care."

"Can't say I do, either. Gage was trying to get me to join this online platform a few weeks back so that we could share pictures and videos back and forth like our own camera roll. I'm clearly getting old, because I had no idea what the hell I was doing on it."

Dexter was quiet when we reached the

top step. I waited for him to pick a direction, but when he didn't, I grew a little worried.

"You okay?"

"You kind of talk about him a lot," he blurted out.

That had me blinking in surprise.

Shit, did I really?

Jesus, this whole time I was trying not to be obvious with my relationship by keeping my hands to myself and this whole time it was my *mouth* that got me in trouble.

"Uh."

What did I even say to him?

Yeah, it's just because we're best friends?

Calling Gage anything like my best friend or whatever felt too small on the scale of what I felt for him. He was *so much* more than that. He was my confidant, my heart, my rock. Our relationship extended past the boundaries of mere labels at this point.

How could I hope to convey that, though, without sounding like an absolutely lunatic?

Especially to my seventeen year old.

"Are... you guys..." Dexter was struggling to get the words out.

A pit in my stomach formed. "We're... uh."

Fuck.

This was like trying to have the damn birds and the bees talk.

Why was this so fucking awkward?

I wanted my son to get to know me, just as I did him. I'd never considered that this would be torturously cringy to speak my true feelings for the man that I was in love with.

He watched me with a pinched expression.

Sighing, I said, "We're dating, Dex."

He nodded slowly. "How long?"

"A year... just about."

He blinked a few times. "Oh."

I slapped my hand to the side of my face to rub at it, scratching a finger through my beard. Hopefully, my cheeks weren't too red. "Yeah."

His expression was morphing into more of a curious one while he watched me carefully. Whatever was going on inside of his head had to be a million questions. He knew I was gay, but he hadn't said what he felt about it outside of him expressing how much it'd hurt Kate, and him by proxy.

Coming face to face with the reality of

something like that was different than hearing it and never having to witness it. It wouldn't surprise me if he asked me to get him on a plane tonight and let him go back home to the safety of heteronormativity. That was more comfortable, even if I had my suspicions about him yesterday.

He made a small humming sound before pivoting on his heel and heading down the hallway behind him. I followed after him, my stomach tight with knots. He shoved a hand into his pocket and pulled out a neatly folded up bundle of papers, un-creasing them with his hand a few times.

"Up ahead is the tech wing. It's supposed to be state of the art." He was talking while his head was buried in the papers—maps, I realized when I got close enough.

"Dex..."

He continued to talk like he hadn't even heard me. "I'm not that well-versed in technology. But I'd like to learn a thing or two. They even have a robotics team."

"Dexter."

He stopped short, turning to look at me. "What?"

I sighed. "Talk to me."

Please.

The answering frown was the least of what I was expecting. "I'm kind of hurt you didn't tell me."

"Hurt?" I repeated.

"Yeah, I—" His gaze darted away from mine, focusing on the hallway we'd stopped right in front of. "I know mom doesn't really care to know... or you didn't want to tell her. I understand that. But..."

My heart softened. "I didn't think you wanted to know, either."

Thankfully, he looked at me again. "I'm not like her, dad."

That hit me hard. I hadn't meant to treat him the same way I did his mom—at arm's length. I wanted our bond to be so much different and here I was, doing what I did to Kate without even trying to meet him halfway and see if he was at all interested.

"Yeah, I go to church. Or, well, I did," he flinched but went on. "But that doesn't mean I hate gay people. I told you I didn't care about it when you told me."

"I know," I said softly. "But hearing about it and seeing it are two different things. I didn't want to freak you out."

Dexter rolled his eyes at me. "You really think you kissing someone is going to freak me out? Trust me, you're not as bad as mom and Dan."

Okay, we'll unpack that later.

"I'm sorry, Dex."

"Were you seriously never going to tell me?" The hurt in his eyes was killing me.

"I was... waiting for the right time." A total lie. Even as I said it, I knew that it was.

Keeping things from my son, even out of paternal instinct, was what got us here in the first place. We'd had a rift between us because I'd kept my distance from him after everything with his mother, believing that I was protecting him while hurting us both in the process.

How was any of that fair?

Yet, I was still doing it.

"Okay, so when was the right time going to be? When we got back on the plane? You know you guys are, like, *really* obvious, right?"

That made me wince. "Sorry…"

He rolled his eyes again. "I'm not trying to be an asshole. I… okay, I know that this is hard to talk to me about. I get that. But aren't we supposed to be trying the honesty thing?"

"Yeah, of course we are."

"So then talk to me? A year is kind of a big deal, dad."

This time I slapped both of my hands over my face and I groaned into them. "I know…"

"That's kind of a marriage time limit."

"What?"

He shrugged at me when I peeked at him through my hands.

"Isn't the saying, if it's been a year, you should know if you want to marry the person you're dating?"

Marriage?

I hadn't thought about that since Kate and I divorced.

Was that true?

Was Gage expecting that?

Neither of us had talked about tying the knot, mostly due to us being long distance for the time being.

That was currently our biggest hurdle to overcome, which wouldn't be getting resolved until I knew where Dexter was going. If he decided on LSU, great. I'd most likely move down here to be with Gage.

If not?

We'd figure something else out.

We'd come this damn far—even if the distance was killing us both.

"Uh…" I dropped my hands to my side.

"We haven't really talked about it."

His lips parted at the same time that his brows pulled together. "Seriously?"

"What?" Now I was feeling a little defensive.

Why the hell was I trying to defend myself to my damn seventeen year old?

"Enough talking about my relationship. Don't we have a school to tour?"

Marching around him, I planted both of my hands on his shoulder blades to guide him down the hallway we were facing. This was a good excuse to get my bearings back, anyway. Coming on this school tour with him hadn't prepared me for the onslaught of fucking questions he'd needle me with about me and Gage.

"Dad." He craned his neck back to look at me.

"How about this," I offered. "I'll tell you about Gage and I while we walk. Sound good?"

For the first time since yesterday, he smiled. "All right, deal."

CHAPTER FIFTEEN

Xavier

BY THE TIME we got back to Gage's, I was both mentally and physically exhausted.

"I'm going to take a shower," Dexter said, moving around me as soon as he kicked his shoes off. "I'm sweaty from walking up and down all those stairs."

"Take your time. Whatever Gage is bringing back will probably need time to heat up, anyway."

He nodded and then headed for the hallway. The bathroom door clicked shut a moment later, leaving me to my own thoughts for the time being. Stumbling over to the couch, I threw myself back on it and let my body sink into the soft cushions.

Who fucking knew divulging my relationship to my teenaged son would have me feeling like I'd just walked out of an intense therapy session?

Though, I guess in a way, it kind of was.

Purging myself from all of the secrets I'd been keeping from him about Gage— all PG, of course—had felt nice. Like a weight was slowly being lifted off of me. But now that everything was out in the open, I was having to deal with the aftermath of letting myself be so vulnerable.

Dexter had taken it well, asking me questions practically after every story I'd told him. It surprised me how much of an interest he'd taken in the subject. Then again, that could be him fishing for answers for his own self.

He still hadn't opened up to me about anything, but I felt like, in due time, he would. Coming home today, I felt a lot closer to him, and like he understood me better than he had when we'd first stepped off of that plane.

The front door opened up, coupled with the sound of a key ring full of keys jingling. I slid my eyes closed in time with the door, the familiar sounds of Gage setting his stuff down by the door filling my ears.

I heard him chuckle when he came into the living room, his soft footsteps wandering over to me. A weight was then settled on top of my chest, his warm body laying on me while his leg hooked over mine.

"Long day?" he teased.

I popped my eyes open. "You don't know the half of it."

He kissed me sweetly, his lips lingering on mine for a moment. "You guys didn't get into an argument, did you?"

"No, nothing like that."

He relaxed visibly. "Okay, good."

He's a good man.

Those words were going to haunt me forever in the best of ways. Honestly, I should've picked up on it then what Dexter was trying to tell me. His approval meant a hell of a lot.

"He knows about us," I said.

Gage's eyes widened. "You told him?"

"Nope."

His mouth opened and closed a few times, a wince pinching his face. "Were we... that obvious?"

"According to him we were. I thought we were being good."

"Me too!"

I laughed. "Maybe he's got exceptional gaydar."

Gage groaned, burying his face in my chest. "I swear, I was only making goo-goo eyes at you when he wasn't looking..."

I ran my fingers through his hair, curling them around the soft locks that had grown longer since the last time we'd seen each other. I liked his hair a little on the longer side. It framed his face perfectly and gave him more of a softer side.

"You want to know what he told me?" When Gage nodded, I said, "He told me that he knew the second you met us in the airport. Apparently, he'd had his suspicions before that and confirmed it then."

He groaned again, turning his face to the side. "It was that damn sign, wasn't it? I knew I should've made it smaller."

He preened when I scratched his scalp gently with my nails. "I think it was more than the sign, babe."

"Was he upset?"

"No, surprisingly. The entire campus tour we talked about it."

"No shit?" When he lifted his head from my chest, he was grinning. "Does that mean we got the gold star of approval?"

"I hope so. He was pretty upset that I didn't tell him about it. He even gave me a lecture about how at the one year mark, I should think about proposing." I laughed.

Thinking that he'd laugh along with me, he surprised me when all he said to that was a soft, "Oh."

That sobered me right up. "Have *you* thought about getting married?"

"To you?"

"Who else?" Trying to tease him again to lighten up the rapidly declining mood, I said, "You got someone else I don't know about?"

"No, no. Nothing like that."

What the hell was going on?

"Gage."

The sound of the bathroom door popping open had him springing off my chest and back onto his feet. His uniform was wrinkled from the way he was laying on me, a deep line formed right across his chest, over his heart.

"I should get lunch started," was all he said, before spinning on his heel and heading into the kitchen.

Sitting up slowly, I stared after him.

What the hell was *that*?

CHAPTER SIXTEEN

Gage

STUPID FUCKING IDIOT.

The mantra I'd been chanting to myself over the past three hours since coming back from lunch.

Seriously, could I ruin a more perfect moment with my dumbass insecurities?

Xavier's wonderful news should've had me jumping over the fucking moon to hear, yet all I'd focused on was the way his face had looked when he'd joked about getting married to me.

That's because he doesn't want *to marry you.*

A groan bubbled up my throat. Picking up the gear bag at my feet, I launched it across the training room, over to where the other ones were stacked.

Why the hell did I care if Xavier didn't want to marry me?

His first marriage had gone to shit, so there were plenty of reasons to not want to do that again.

Sure, it would be different if he was married to someone he was *actually* attracted to, but sometimes people didn't want to chance it. That didn't mean that that person wasn't in love with their partner. It just meant they had reservations about legally binding their life to another's.

"You good in here?" Quinn wandered into the room.

"Yep." I chucked another bag across the room. "What's up?"

"You're making a lot of noise in here. Thought I might have to come rescue you from the pile burying you alive."

I scoffed. "Yeah, if only."

I'd welcome a fucking tower of gear falling on top of me right now and taking me out. It'd save me the damn embarrassment of having to go back home after this and face my boyfriend and his confused expressions while I tried to pretend none of this ever happened.

Why I felt the need to get all up in my feelings about a hypothetical situation was beyond me. We'd never discussed marriage before this—never even had the option on the damn table. The second that door was no longer there, though, I'd gotten butt hurt about it.

And for what?

To torture myself?

Xavier and I were *good*. We were *happy*.

Why couldn't that be enough for my stupid ass brain to comprehend?

"Uh oh." Quinn planted himself right on top of the next bag before I could grab it. "Trouble in paradise?"

Annoyed, I said, "Can you move?"

"Not until you spill the beans, Torres."

"Quinn," I growled.

He simply flashed me a pleasant smile. "Come on, you know you want to tell me."

"Don't you have someone else to pick on?"

"Nah, it's his day off. So I need to fill

the void somehow."

This was so fucking typical of him. If he didn't have Jase around to bug, he'd sniff out the weakest link in the chain until he found someone to attach to for the rest of the day. Which just so happened to be me.

Honestly, I didn't have much fight left in me. I was already exhausted from doing mental gymnastics in my head, trying to convince myself that I wasn't crazy in feeling justified over my reaction to Xavier, while at the same time feeling bad about it.

What did that say about me?

About us?

He had enough on his plate to deal with without me adding to it with my stupid lovesick heart bleeding at the mere possibility that marriage wasn't in our future. He hadn't said it out loud but his face had told me plenty.

Wandering over to one of the metal chairs set back against the wall, I flopped down onto it while I leaned forward and rested my head in my hands. Overthinking was my specialty.

And when it came to Xavier?

Forget it. I was cooked.

"Come on, man. Talk to me," Quinn said.

"You can't tell anyone."

"Uh..."

Rolling my eyes, I said. "Besides Jase."

"You got yourself a deal."

I sighed, my gaze directed at the floor. "So, my boyfriend's up from California visiting and earlier when I went home for lunch, he and I got to talking about some things. And... I don't know. I guess I took it a little more personally than he probably meant it to come across."

"I'm loving the cryptic way you're telling me this, Torres."

Ugh.

I let my hands drop from my head when I lifted it up. "We got onto the topic of marriage."

His brows shot up to his hairline. "Wow, congrats. That's pretty serious."

"Yeah, except he laughed in my face about it."

"Yikes."

"I feel like a total idiot. This is the first time it was ever brought up and I froze. He was joking around about it. Meanwhile, I took it seriously and got my own feelings hurt."

"Hmm." Quinn leaned back on the bag, his body shifting slightly. He ran one of his hands over his jaw a few times while he chose his words carefully. "So what exactly did he say to you? I'm just trying to get the full picture here."

"Apparently, his kid was saying that after a year, you should really start thinking about marriage. And I guess Xavier found that kind of funny and joked with me about it."

"Did he *say* he didn't want to get married?"

"Well, he's been married before."

"That's not exactly answering my question," Quinn said.

"His face told me plenty."

"I think I see what's going on." He lifted himself up from the bag and headed over to me, hands on his hips. "You got all up in your head again."

That had me frowning.

He went on. "Gage, you gotta stop doing that. You're getting your own feelings hurt and there's probably no reason for it. What if he *does* want marriage in the future?"

"You should've seen his face, man. It wasn't—he thought it was ridiculous."

"Maybe you just filled in the blanks for him," he suggested.

Frustration was rising in my chest.

It felt like I was talking in circles. I knew what I saw when I was watching Xavier talk to me about it. His tone, the way he phrased things. All of it, coupled with his expression when he'd asked me if *I* thought about marriage was like all one big joke to him.

Why wouldn't it be when the last time he was bound to someone legally, it ended in a flaming pile of shit?

If I were in Xavier's shoes, I'd run for the damn hills anytime someone mentioned the 'M' word to me.

"Yo! Gage!" Zander's face appeared in the doorway. "You got a couple of guests out here waiting for you."

My stomach flipped.

Probably Xavier here with Dexter to tour the place.

Now that his son knew we were dating, he was probably going around on a grand tour of all my usual spots. On any other normal day, I'd be hyped to show them both around the place I spent ninety-nine percent of my time at.

Today, I was tempted to hide in the bathroom and beg Quinn and Zander to make up some excuse as to why I wasn't here.

Dragging myself up from my chair with

a sigh, I shuffled out to the hallway and followed Zander back to the main garage. A few of my coworkers were all gathered around one of the front side doors, most likely welcoming Xavier and Dexter in.

Captain Clarke was nowhere to be seen, which was out of the norm for him when it came to new guests at the fire station. Usually, he was first on scene.

Quinn slapped his hands on my shoulders from behind me and steered me toward the group, speeding me up from how I'd been dragging my feet along the concrete floor. As soon as we reached them, the group parted, smiling faces all turning to face me.

In the middle of it all was *not* my boyfriend and his teenaged kid.

But my *own brothers*.

Instantly, my eyes began to water.

"What the..."

"Surprise!" Greyson grinned, throwing his arms around me first. Over his shoulder, I could see Asher smiling at us in amusement, holding a medium-sized box in his arms.

I wrapped Greyson up in a tight hug, not believing that he was actually here in the damn flesh. That *either* of them were.

"When the hell did you guys get in?" I said. "When did you get time off?"

And how the hell did they coordinate behind my back?

As Greyson pulled away, he stepped to the side while snagging the box from his brother's hold. Asher came next, hugging me tight enough to practically snap my bones in half.

"We wanted to surprise you," he said in my ear.

Well, they sure as hell succeeded.

Out of any kind of surprise they could've given me, *this* was by far the best one. I'd spent the last two weeks lamenting about spending the holidays by myself and here these two were—conspiring behind my back like the lovable little shits they were.

Asher stepped back from our hug, a wide smile resting on his face. His hair was longer and shaggier than when I last saw him, while his brother's was shaved back to a military cut.

They both looked good.

Happy.

Healthy.

Just how I'd wanted them to be.

"Aw, a happy family reunion!" Ellie clapped. "The Captain's going to be thrilled. You guys are coming to the

Christmas party, right?"

The twins exchanged a look.

"Is there free food?" Asher asked. "If so, count me in."

"Ditto," his brother quickly replied.

"Hey, my kinda guys." Quinn offered them both a high five.

"Funny," I said and then nodded to the box. "What's all that?"

Greyson hid behind his twin. "You can't open it until Christmas."

Oh boy... that didn't give off a foreboding feeling or anything. The last time my brothers surprised me with something and refused to let me open it until Christmas morning, I'd gotten a lovely prank spring-loaded whipped pie to the face and two newly turned teenagers cackling endlessly while they recorded the entire thing.

Now that they were actually adults with *real adult money,* I couldn't even imagine what was waiting for me inside of that mystery box.

"We've got our bags outside," Asher said, gesturing to the side door. "We took a rideshare here from the airport."

"I can't believe you two got your flights to come in at the same time and got all the way here without me knowing." As much as I was impressed with their planning, I was damn proud, too. Look how independent I'd taught them to be!

"Asher's plane didn't get in for a few hours, so I was stuck waiting in one of the terminal chairs." Greyson raised his hands above his head, stretching long enough that there was an audible pop that had his body relaxing instantly. "I can't wait to sleep in an actual bed for once."

Oh shit.

"Uh, actually…" Fuck, I totally forgot about my guests. "That might be a problem."

Asher laughed. "I told you he turned your room into an office. You owe me five bucks."

"No way." Greyson's eyes met mine. "You didn't, did you?"

"No!"

"He's definitely lying," Zander said, ever the pot-stirrer.

What the hell.

"I didn't."

"Wait, I thought your boyfriend was up?" Quinn asked, his brows knitting together in confusion, most likely rethinking our entire earlier conversation.

To my left, Ellie gasped. "You got your

boyfriend to come visit? He can come to the party!"

Oh. My. God.

"Guys."

"Wait, hold up. Does this mean we actually get to meet him?" Greyson asked.

This was like them teasing me when I'd first told them that I was dating Xavier all over again. "Can you guys be normal about this?"

"No way," Asher said.

Of course.

Why would they be?

They were my baby brothers and under strict sibling obligations to make fun of me until I was dead. Even then, they'd probably be pranking me over my damn casket one last time until I was lowered into the dirt.

"At least try and be on your best

behavior," I said. "He's got his son with him. I told them they could stay at the house while they toured LSU this weekend."

"Oh shit, he's a sport's guy?" Greyson asked.

"No? Not exactly."

Asher nodded sagely. "Academics. Respect."

I rolled my eyes. Whatever that meant.

"Anyway, they're there now. I get off here in twenty minutes, so I'll drive us all back. You guys hang here while I go finish what I was doing. Sound good?"

Both of them threw me a thumbs up. "Roger that."

Oh boy, this was going to be interesting.

CHAPTER SEVENTEEN

Xavier

RECEIVING THE FRANTIC text of *'hey my brothers surprised me at the fire station'* was probably the last thing I expected to see when I grabbed my phone to check my notifications on the off chance that Kate had called me.

I was glad that things worked out for Gage and his brothers, and was happy that my intuition about them had been correct. He'd put way too much love and care into them for them to turn around and write him off in order to experience living on their own for a little bit longer.

The holidays were a special time for most families. Coming together in order to celebrate that was more meaningful than a lot of people realized. I'm glad the boys weren't taking that for granted.

Time was so short and life was full of unpredictable ups and downs.

There was no guarantee that there would be another day, so why chance it?

"Hey, Dex?" I called from the living room.

A minute later, he popped his head out from the doorway of his room.

"Gage's brothers surprised him at the station. You mind bunking with me so they can have one of their rooms back?"

He gave me a funny look. "I guess..."

"It's just temporary."

He was quiet for a moment, his expression growing more perplexed. "I'm surprised you're not going to room with Gage? Unless they also don't know..."

"No..." My voice sounded a little strangled while I spoke. "They do."

"Okay, so..."

I rubbed at my cheeks, feeling them grow hot to the touch.

Who would've thought my own kid would be suggesting I bunk with my boyfriend while on a father-son trip?

This entire time, I thought he'd balk at the idea of him finding out I had a boyfriend, let alone bringing him to his house to crash while on our trip.

"I just think it would be easier," Dexter explained.

"No, yeah. You're right. I didn't want you to feel uncomfortable."

He shrugged. "It's not that I don't want to share a room with you. But I value my privacy to wind down at night."

"No worries." Honestly, I got that more than he knew. Decompressing after a long day of people-ing was the only way I wasn't driven to insanity on a daily basis.

It seemed that Dexter had inherited my introverted nature. Not surprising, considering we were similar in more ways than our looks. He was smart like Kate, driven like me, and intuitive like the both of us.

He was a perfect blend of us both in the best way—the only thing good we'd ever done together.

"We'll work something out," I said.

"Yeah, let me know."

Right then, the front door to Gage's house unlocked and opened, voices filtering in from outside.

"I'm telling you, I'll win in an arm wrestling competition any day of the week. I lift eighty pound bags of feed every day."

"And *I'm* telling *you,* I'm in the goddamn military. I lift that shit for breakfast."

"Hello, you're a medic?"

"Okay, and I still have fitness tests to pass?"

Ah, that must be the twins.

Lifting myself up from the couch, I headed for the front door to greet them. Dexter ducked back into his room to hide, probably overwhelmed by their loud voices. I could sympathize in a sense—it wasn't my forte to entertain a bunch of extroverts, but at least I had Gage as a buffer.

Who did Dexter have?

Me?

I didn't know these two, either, so I'd be just as lost as a buffer, if not worse than not having one to begin with.

Making my way through the living room and into the small foyer, I spotted the twins lingering in the doorway. Both of them had large duffels swung over their shoulders, one of them with a military print.

Behind them, Gage was stepping up into the house, waving his hands for them to clear the doorway while he dragged another bag in through the door. He let out a loud huff of air when letting go of the strap, straightening back up to brush his hands together.

"All right. That's everything," he said.

"Nice," one of the twins said, swinging the door closed behind him.

All at once, the three of them turned to me. A long beat of silence fell over us all as they took me in, their eyes curious while Gage shifted awkwardly on his feet.

One of the twins pointed at me. "Hey, it's you."

"In the flesh," I said, heading over to them to grab the bag Gage had lugged inside.

It was heavy as fuck when I got a hold of it.

What the hell had these two brought home, fucking bricks?

"Wow, you're way taller than I expected," one of them said. "Gage, you got a type."

"Shut up," he gritted through his

teeth, face on fire.

"Oh really..." Sue me for being curious, but I had to know. "Do tell."

I was never one to get jealous, but when it came to Gage, all bets were off. I'd never go out of my way to beat someone up if I caught them flirting with him, but that didn't mean I wouldn't be marking my territory with a heated kiss or something similar.

Call me a caveman.

The twin with the shorter hair laughed. "We have stories for days. You want to hear what it was like when he had a crush on the cashier at the mini-mart down the road? Oh, or how about that time he was trying to hit on the guy at the gas station who was buying a bunch of junk food 'cause he had the munchies and could barely understand Gage because he was so high."

"Greyson. Shut up," Gage choked out.

Oh, this was too good. "You guys up for long? I've got all weekend."

They both grinned at me.

"Hey, I like him," the one with the longer hair said, nudging Gage in the ribs.

"Asher," Gage said in a monotone, gesturing to one twin and then the other. "Greyson. This is Xavier. *Behave.*"

"It's nice to meet you two," I said.

"Likewise," they both said at the same time.

"I'm so sorry ahead of time," Gage said to me.

"I think you might be needing that sentiment more than me."

He answered me with a groan.

"Wait, where's your little dude?" Greyson said, glanced around.

"He's taking a breather." Forcing my kid to be social kind of felt wrong, especially after the intense morning we'd had. If he wanted to hide for a bit while these two got settled, I wasn't going to tell him no.

Greyson nodded sagely. "Respect."

Behind him, Gage rolled his eyes. "Okay, you two. Stop interrogating him. You're going to scare him off."

My face twisted into a smile. Not likely, but they could damn well try. I had a feeling we were going to get along fine. I had a few tricksters to deal with back home, so this wasn't much different. As long as they respected Dexter, we'd be all good.

"You guys have a long flight?" I asked, leading them back into the living room.

"Not too bad," Asher answered first.

"Grey had to wait for my plane to land while I got to sleep like a baby on my flight over."

"I hate that you can pass out on anything even remotely comfortable," his brother said, tossing his bag down by the hallway leading back to the bedrooms.

"I think the word you're looking for is 'envy'."

I felt an arm snake around my waist from behind, tugging me back while the boys headed for the kitchen together. Gage nuzzled his face into my neck, breathing me in while he had a tight hold of me.

"Quite the surprise," I said once we were alone.

He kissed my neck. "You okay with this?"

"Your house, babe."

He nipped at my skin. "Be serious."

"I am. I'm glad they're here. I had a feeling they'd surprise you, actually."

"Really?" Gage pulled back from me, a bemused expression falling over his face. "What gave it away?"

"You raised them."

His eyes shimmered slightly. "Aw, stop. That's the nicest thing anyone has ever said."

I couldn't help but reach over and cup his face, pulling him into a chaste kiss. "I mean it. Your giant heart reflects in them."

"Ugh." He leaned into me again. "I love you."

Whatever our weirdness from before was about, I was glad that it'd seemingly been forgotten about. I had half a mind to ask him about it while we were alone and in our own little bubble, however, spoiling the mood in order to talk about something that seemed a little more serious felt wrong.

I'd bring it up to him before we left, for sure. For now, though, I wanted us to enjoy the time we had together now that there was going to be a full house.

The soft sound of a throat being cleared had us both untangling ourselves immediately. Dexter was standing just beyond the start of the hallway, his eyes averted while he squinted at the wall.

Jesus, to go from us not touching each other in front of him to getting caught practically making out—how fucking embarrassing. We really needed to get it together.

"Dexter!" Gage clapped his hands together. "How was your campus tour?

Did you like it?"

He cleared his throat again. "Good. Fine. Walked a lot."

Gage nodded slowly with a forced smile. "That sounds fun. Er, I'm glad it went well."

The sound of something crashing in the kitchen had us all whipping around toward the noise, a faint 'oops' following right after.

"Oh my god," Gage mumbled, storming into the kitchen.

Maybe Gage would have his hands too full for us to get caught like this again. The thought was a little depressing, considering all I wanted to do was touch and hold him, but if it saved us from an awkward situation like this, then I was all for it.

Turning to my son, he slowly wandered

over to me. "They seem... excitable."

"Yeah. Look, Dex, I'm sorry—"

He cut me off. "Can I tell you something?"

I was scared to ask. "Yes?"

Dexter shook his head at me. "You got it bad."

I held back a guilty smile.

I really, really did.

CHAPTER EIGHTEEN

Xavier

TO BOTH MY and Gage's surprise, the boys got along swimmingly.

Over dinner, there was a bit of a tense debate over who was the first allowed to cut the pre-made turkey Gage had bought and heated up from the store. But once Dexter had won the impromptu rock, paper, scissors battle he'd been roped into, everything settled into a comfortable rhythm, as if we'd been doing this kind of tradition for years.

I enjoyed seeing my son bonding with kids around his age. With both Asher and Greyson out of the house and out living their lives, it gave Dexter a good insight into what was to come once he was officially graduated and old enough to do the same.

Getting ready for that transition in life made me nauseous, despite Gage's numerous hand squeezes under the table every time Dexter talked about going to some far away school that would be at least a plane ride away.

I had to settle with myself that it was okay that my son was going to be spreading his wings and flying from the nest soon. All parents had to deal with it eventually. Hell, Gage was already through the thick of it and barely surviving. If we didn't have each other, we'd be sunk by now.

That part comforted me, at least. We had each other to lean on while our hearts were out traveling the world without us.

"All right, clean up time," Gage sang out as he got up from his chair.

The twins were on their feet instantly, collecting everyone's finished plates and stacking them to take into the kitchen to wash. Dexter and I followed suit, grabbing the leftover food to bring into the kitchen for Gage to wrap up and save for tomorrow.

"Thank you," Gage whispered in my ear as I passed the plate of half-eaten turkey to him. I knew he was thanking me for more than helping him clean up.

My heart squeezed in my chest, the sincerity for whatever he was referring to quite obvious in the way his eyes twinkled as he smiled at me. Too bad we weren't alone or else I'd back him right up into that counter and have my wicked way with him.

"You into video games, Dexter?" Greyson asked, scraping off one of the plates into the garbage next to the sink.

"I play sometimes. I don't have a lot of friends that are into the kind I like," he said, passing another plate over.

"What are you into?" Asher asked.

"You know those simulator games that are realistic where you do mundane tasks that you'd otherwise hate to do in the real world?"

Greyson kicked his twin in the shin. "Dude, you *have* to show him that farming simulator one you have.”

Asher nodded quickly. “You’re going to love it. You get to farm crops from a field.”

How the hell was that *a fun video game idea?*

Honestly, I’d never understand the younger generation. Half of the shit they found entertaining baffled me.

Dexter turned to me with those big doe-eyes of his, silently pleading for me to let him go hang out with the older boys.

How could I possibly say no to a look like that?

I snagged the stack of plates from him. “Just remember, we’ve got the rest of your itinerary tomorrow.”

“I’ll set an alarm,” he said, and then followed the twins out of the kitchen, abandoning Gage and I to the rest of clean-up duty.

Gage snorted. "You sucker."

"I know." Setting the plates down on the counter, I brushed my hands on the towel next to the sink before cupping his face with my hands and bringing him in for a kiss. "Would you believe me if I told you I did that for this?"

He smiled. "You *sucker.*"

"Only for you." I kissed him again, this time deepening it.

Delightfully dangerous of us to be doing this with our kids mere feet from us in the room next door. At the same time, I had no self-control when Gage was around me. He could simply *breathe* in my direction and I was popping a boner that acted like a fucking compass pointing right at him.

I'm sure there would be a point in time when this enhanced tension between us would die down and we'd eventually fall into a comfortable rhythm of being old and gray together.

Until that time came around, though, I was riding this out for as long as possible. Call me selfish for leaning into my rabid desire for this man. It was more likely that I was on the 'crazy' side of the spectrum than anything else.

Gage moaned softly against my mouth, turning us so that he had his back resting against the counter. His hands came up to rest on my chest, pushing gently until we parted from our kiss. His face was flushed in that beautiful way it always was after a heated kiss, which only made me want to kiss him that much more.

"Xavier..." His pupils were blown as he looked at me. "I have a question for you."

"If it's 'can you fuck me against this

counter' the answer is yes."

He laughed, slapping my chest. "Nice try. We'll get caught for sure. I don't know about you, but I really don't want to have to deal with the aftermath of the boys walking in on that."

"True." More than likely they'd avoid the kitchen, and us, like the plague. But his point remained the same. I *also* didn't want to irreversibly scar my kid. "What's up?"

"So... there's this holiday party going on at the station."

I waited for him to finish. When he didn't, I said, "Okay? You have to go help out after this or something?"

"No, no. Nothing like that." He rubbed my chest. "I was thinking that, since you and Dexter are here, you could both come to it? It's not for another week, but I heard Dexter saying he doesn't start school again until after New Years."

"I'd love to..." His eyes lit up instantly, which made me feel bad for immediately saying afterward. "But I have to bring Dex back home to his mom for Christmas."

"Oh..."

I squeezed his sides. "Maybe next year."

"You can't come back or anything? I don't mind paying for a plane ticket for you."

"That's sweet, Gage. But you should be spending the holiday with your family."

He mumbled something under his breath while pulling away from me.

"What was that?"

He shook his head. "Nothing. Never mind. Forget I said anything."

Confusion rattled in my brain, much

like it had when he'd pulled away from me earlier when he'd come home for lunch.

What was going on?

I'd never seen him act this way. I'd blame it on his brothers being here, but he hadn't even known they'd been on their way during lunch.

This wasn't like Gage. He was usually the talker and I was the listener. He never shied away from expressing himself or his feelings, but right now this felt like pulling teeth from him.

"Hey…" I grabbed onto his arm. "Talk to me."

"It's fine. I get it."

"Get what?" I asked.

"It's just a stupid party. My coworkers were all bugging me about bringing you."

Shit.

"I'm sorry. I wish I could. Kate's going

to want Dex there for Christmas and she'll probably let me have him right after, so I don't want to miss that."

"I get it, Xavier. You don't need to explain things to me like I'm a child."

His arm slipped from my grip.

I silently watched him as he grabbed one of the plates and scraped off the food remnants before dunking it in the pre-filled sink. His movements were methodical and robotic, like he'd put himself on autopilot without even thinking about it.

My stomach hurt with how hard the knot in it was clenching. We'd never really had a situation where we weren't seeing eye-to-eye outside of a work thing. We'd disagreed plenty while he'd been training with me, but outside of that, we were usually on the same page.

Me being sober had made our communications skills even better.

So what the fuck was this, then?

"Gage," I said slowly. "What's happening?"

"I don't know what you mean." He dunked another plate, tossing the fork into the sink with a quick flick of his wrist.

"What did I say?"

He sighed at me. "Nothing, Xavier. Drop it."

How the hell was I supposed to drop it when there was obviously a gigantic cloud of tension looming over us?

We never did this—we weren't like this. Ever since this afternoon, we'd been in this weird spot that I had no fucking clue how we even got into in the first place.

If I did, I would've fixed it by now.

"Baby," I tried again, reaching for him.

He dodged me, moving around to the other side of the trash to toss the last of the plate scrapings into it. "It's fine. Just forget about it."

"I can't when you're upset with me."

"I'm not."

"You are. Unless I'm fucking blind and there's a third person in this kitchen right now." I furrowed my brows, setting my lips into a thin line.

He lifted his gaze up from the trash to give me a look. "Funny."

There had to be more to this than just the party. There was no way he'd be getting this upset that I couldn't come to a work function.

Disappointed?

Sure.

But upset?

No way.

Gage was way more levelheaded than that.

He was the one to get me to actually get in touch with my own emotions and begin to untangle the absolute fucking mess that was my trauma. *He* convinced me to take my sobriety seriously because it was either that or lose my kid.

Gage wasn't the kind of guy to let his emotions run rampant and wild. He was one of the most regulated people I knew.

A little anxious at times?

Who wasn't these days?

We had stressful jobs that were constantly putting us in life or death situations.

Anxiety kind of came with the territory.

This was something way bigger than that. It had to be, or else I was going fucking crazy.

Clearly, he wasn't up to talking about it, no matter how many times I could try weaseling it out of him.

But was this the kind of situation that I let drop and forget about it?

Or did I give him the space he needed to figure out his own emotions before he could actually talk to me about them?

I wasn't sure. Not without asking him, but that was obviously out of the question. Right now, the best that I could offer was a listening ear when he was ready. Until then, I was going to have to suck it up and wait it out until he came to me.

Whenever the fuck that happened.

Bridging the distance between us, I wrapped my arms around him from behind and pressed a soft kiss to his neck. "Come find me later, okay?"

So we can talk.

He nodded silently, working overtime at scrubbing the plate in his hands.

With a sigh, I dropped my arms and stepped away, giving him the space he clearly needed to decompress from this. My heart was heavy as I left the kitchen, and him, behind.

In the living room, the boys were crowded around the giant TV, all of them sitting on the floor and craning their necks up while some kind of video game was playing. I stood behind the couch and watched for a second, trying to distract myself from going back in and begging Gage to talk to me.

"Nice. See that pasture where all the wheat is? Mow over it so you can start making barrels to sell at the market,"

Asher was saying, pointing to the screen.

"Got it," Dexter replied. The tractor on the screen slowly puttered over to a different colored field with a very realistic sounding engine.

"Nice. It's double drops," Greyson said. "That'll be perfect when you sell your first few barrels. You can buy a longer attachment so you can farm larger areas."

Shaking my head, I stepped away from the living room and headed down the hall to my bedroom, or rather, one of the twin's. Packing all my things up and zipping my bag, I carried it into Gage's room to set it down on his bed.

Following Dexter's suggestion of bunking with Gage was a smarter idea than forcing him to share a bed with me. After all, I'd be sneaking off to see him anyway after what just happened. Might as well kill two birds with one stone.

Heading back to the other room, I quickly changed the sheets on the bed and fluffed up the pillows nice and neat until I was satisfied with what I was leaving behind.

I swung the door shut behind me before making my way back to Gage's room. I had a hunch that he was going to avoid me for as long as possible. Which meant that I was either going to have to drag him to bed, or he was going to pretend like everything was fine and try to go to sleep in order to avoid this conversation.

Both options had me feeling nauseous.

Lifting my bag up from the bed, I let it fall to the floor at my feet and kicked it to press flush against the wall out of the way of the main walkway. I grabbed my phone out of my pocket, and Kate's name flashed across my screen.

Have Dexter call me, please, was all her text said.

Groaning, I let my body fall back onto the bed, bouncing slightly from the sudden weight fluctuation. If Kate was going to demand Dexter to come home a day early, I was going to actually lose it.

No, scratch that.

The more likely scenario was that I would be calling her up and demanding to know why the hell she was cutting our three-day weekend short when I'd been asking for very little from her from the beginning.

Lifting my phone up closer to my face, I typed out a quick *'sure'* and sent it on its way.

I let myself wallow for a total of five

entire minutes before forcing myself up from the bed and heading out of the bedroom to go find Dexter.

CHAPTER NINETEEN

Gage

"ANOTHER WEEK?" I overheard Xavier saying from the living room right as I shut the water off for the sink. "That's what she said?"

"You want to call her back and talk to her?" came Dexter's reply.

Snagging the towel off of the rack to dry my now thoroughly pruned hands, I slapped it down onto the counter once I was done with it and headed into the living room. The game on the TV was paused while both the twins were patiently sitting on the floor in front of the couch while Xavier and Dexter were talking.

Xavier had his phone in his hands that he tossed between them every few seconds, a pensive look etched onto his face. "It's just a little surprising, is all…"

Dexter offered his own phone over, waving it slightly in the space between them. "That's all she said to me, but if you want to ask—"

His father was shaking his head, putting both of his hands up in mock surrender. "As long as she's not expecting us back on a flight Monday afternoon."

"What's going on?" I asked.

Xavier let out a soft sigh and then

turned my way. "Kate called." Holding back a grimace should've earned me some kind of award. "And said that we can stay the week if we want."

There's no way I heard that right. "The *whole* week?"

He glanced back at Dexter who merely shrugged. "That's what she told me."

A whole week?!

I'd get Xavier for longer than just these measly three days that could barely even count as an extended weekend since he'd be traveling back home on the third day of it.

Could Kate really be so generous?

Did she have any of those bones left in her body?

I couldn't imagine her calling Dexter up to tell him that she'd done some soul searching and realized that keeping a son from his father was wrong and for them to take their time in getting back to California.

All of it was too good to be true.

Where was the catch?

"If that's okay with you," Xavier was saying, his gaze darting from me, over to the twins. "All of you. I don't want us imposing on anything."

The urge to tell him to shut up and kiss him stupid was itching me right on the back of the neck, hard to ignore while my mind raced with the possibility that my wish of bringing him to the Christmas party would be coming true after all if I could convince Ellie to move the date up.

Sure, they'd be leaving *right* before Christmas day, but I was still getting them for the week leading up to it. That was counting as a win in my book. Even if

XAVIER

I couldn't have Xavier for the entire holiday stretch like I selfishly wanted to.

Oh shit, I needed to go out and buy them both gifts.

What was Dexter into?

I could probably get the boys to weasel some info out of him in order to give me an idea on what to go off of. Xavier was easy—my issue was blowing him out of the water with what I got him, and not just buying him something that he'd tot on for a few days before forgetting altogether in a few months.

A strong hand gripped my shoulder, ripping me out of my thoughts. "Are you okay with this, Gage?"

My gaze snapped to Xavier's, the wariness in them not lost on me.

Our earlier tiff was still hanging in the air between us and not as easily forgotten as I would've liked for it to be. While I wasn't exactly sure why getting so triggered lately by our relationship had been happening, there was still that nagging feeling in me that was telling me something needed to be done.

What that was, I had no fucking clue.

If I dug down deep enough, I was positive that the answer would most likely have something to do with this long distance. Having him so far away from me the vast majority of the time was beginning to wear on me more than I initially suspected, causing these weird rifts that I couldn't seem to stop myself from falling into, and taking him down with me.

Beating out my frustrations on Xavier wasn't fair, especially since he had very limited time with me left—even with the extended few days Kate had apparently granted us with. He was, unfortunately, the closest punching bag that I had and all my brain wanted to do was scream 'fire!' and swing wildly.

The hand tightened on my shoulder once more.

Shaking my head, I said, "Yeah, sorry. It's all good with me."

"You sure?" he asked.

He seemed to be fishing for something—some kind of reassurance that I wasn't simply giving in by being put on the spot. Even with my mood still in a weird place, that was very much appreciated. Getting pressured into doing things for the sake of keeping the peace annoyed me to no end.

"I'm sure. We can work on getting your return tickets sorted out tonight."

Thankfully, he seemed to pick up on the hidden meaning underneath my nicely dressed words. "Why don't we go to that now? Don't need the seats to fill up on us."

"Laptop's in my room." I nodded toward the hallway.

While I dreaded having any kind of conversation that would bring us right back to where we were at in the kitchen, there was also a part of me that needed to purge this toxic shit from my system. Getting it all out in the open—whatever it really was—would get us back on the same page again.

Hopefully.

Xavier smiled at me slightly, his hand dropping back down to his side. "Guess we won't be needing to cram our entire itinerary into tomorrow after all."

At that, Dexter turned to the twins and said, "That means I get to stay up until the sun rises."

"Nice try," Xavier drawled. "You're still going to bed at a reasonable time."

"What's reasonable to you, Xavier?" Greyson asked. "Four am? Five?"

Asher gave him a hard shove on the back. "Yeah, like you'll be able to stay up that long. The military's got you guys in bed as soon as the sun goes down and getting up while it's still dark out."

"Okay. Pot, kettle?" Greyson shot back. "Weren't you the one complaining in the group chat how your boss is constantly waking you up at the ass crack of dawn?"

"Don't see him anywhere around here, now do we?"

"Boys..." I chided. "How about we're in bed by one."

"Fine," they chimed at the same time.

Xavier nodded to Dexter. "You too."

"Sure. Got it," he answered.

Blowing out a breath, I pivoted my body toward the hallway, feeling the energy in the room shift while Xavier followed me and the sounds of the game on the TV came to life again. The boys were good at distracting themselves, giving Xavier plenty of time to talk. However long they roped Dexter into hanging out with them, it would be at least for a little while.

Heading into my room, the first thing I noticed was Xavier's bag by my bed, leaning up against the wall. My lip quirked up involuntarily as my body relaxed at the sight of it. He didn't seem to be too mad at me if he was willing to share a room with me tonight.

XAVIER

That could all be a massive coincidence that aligned with giving the twins back one of their rooms, but I wanted to look at it as Xavier *actually* wanting to spend time with me despite our weirdness.

He shut the door behind us softly once he was inside, turning to me with a pinched expression. "Gage..."

My heart beat solidly in my chest, choking me from saying anything to him.

Expressing myself had never been a problem before. Even as a kid raising my two baby brothers, I'd always expressed exactly what was on my mind. There was never a point in my life where I subscribed to the idea that I had 'nothing to say' about a situation, even if it was a mundane one.

Yet here and now, I was stumbling to

form my words properly to express myself.

How could I when I wasn't able to name what was wrong?

My theory was the distance between us affecting our bond—the issue being that there was no real way to prove that was actually what was going on with me unless he left and I could definitely say that was the real problem and not some bandage over top of the real festering wound.

Not to mention that with Xavier being here now, I should be over the moon wanting to crawl up into his skin while I had him, not picking stupid fights.

Everything was so damn jumbled. Nothing was making sense.

Why did I care if Xavier never married me and chose his family over spending one day out of the year with his family when I had him every other damn time?

Because you want him to be a part of your *family.*

Ugh...

Xavier crept across the room, standing before me with his hands outstretched to cup my face. He stroked his thumbs along my cheeks in a gentle way, soothing me despite my raging whirlwind of thoughts.

I'd always been transparent to him, no matter how well I believed I'd covered up the truth. He saw through me and into my soul like a damn pane of glass.

"Sorry," I whispered.

For everything.

He shook his head and bent forward to press his lips against mine in a chaste kiss. I melted into him instantly, my arms coming up to curl tightly around him as he adjusted his hold on me. He walked me back toward the bed, lowering me down onto it the second the back of my knees brushed up against it.

His body was a solid weight on top of me, comforting in that weighted blanket kind of way. Our kiss was slow, and we took the time to savor the feeling of each other without the feverish need to strip our clothes off and go at it like a couple of wild animals.

This was what made all of the distance and conflicting schedules worth it—having him here with me in this quiet moment with no outside interruptions to rip us apart and force us back into our roles as parents or first responders.

Stressing about him leaving when I should be savoring what little time left I had was only going to make my moods worse and cause further issues that didn't need to be there in the first place. Quinn was right about it all—I was getting too up in my head about things that shouldn't even matter at this point.

What I really needed to be focusing on was soaking up as much time with my boyfriend as possible until he had to go home.

Xavier drifted back from our kiss, his fingers moving from my cheek to trail down my forehead and over my jaw. His treatment of me, like I was some kind of precious piece of ancient pottery, would never cease to get my heart fluttering.

"Talk to me." His voice was soft.

"I miss you," was all I could think to say back. Because at the end of it all, that was the truth. I missed him even when he was here with me.

His expression softened. "I miss you,

too, Gage."

We had a week together.

A whole damn week.

Spending it on dreading the inevitable goodbye was only going to leave me feeling regretful in the end. Xavier would be back; he wasn't leaving me forever no matter what that traitorous voice inside of my head told me.

Regardless of him not wanting to marry me, or not spending Christmas with me, we still had each other. Our bond had been forged in brotherhood during the chopper crash, long before we were officially dating. That wasn't something that could easily be wiped away no matter the circumstances.

Wrapping my limbs around him, I breathed in his woodsy scent and let my eyes close.

XAVIER

I needed to be grateful for what I had before I ended up chasing it away.

CHAPTER TWENTY

Xavier

TWO DAYS AFTER Kate's phone call, Dexter and I found ourselves at LSU's botanical gardens.

The place was absolutely beautiful and only an eight-minute drive from the campus. Arriving at the facility right after lunch, there were already plenty of people milling about in the front area leading into the main entrance.

While waiting in line to get in, we people-watched at the kids with their families running around on the front lawn while parents wrestled bracelet tickets onto their wrists. Simple things like this were the unexpectedly fun parts about coming to a new city.

We'd decided to start off working our way to the back of the property and ending at the front, leaving the flower gardens for last, since that's where most of the tourists that were around for the season were convening.

A good bout of rain had cut the mugginess in the air down by about half, leaving us to walk through the trail in a pleasant sixty-five degrees and sunny. The boardwalk leading back to the wetlands was surrounded by tall trees on either side of it, shading us under a nice canopy from the hot sun above.

Dexter had a map of the entire site in his hands that he stared down at while we walked side-by-side. He'd already marked off a few spots that I took as him wanting to stop by our way down, judging by the stars next to them.

This entire trip, I'd been impressed with his meticulous nature. Not being around for most of his formidable school years had put me at a disadvantage for knowing a key part of my son's life that led him into getting into LSU to begin with.

Seeing him like this was a nice peek into a part of what I'd missed for all of those years he'd moved through school.

"You know, if you end up going to LSU, you'll be able to walk here whenever you want." With this place being as large as it was, I doubted we were going to get the full experience of everything on just today alone.

There was a bit of regret in me for not having researched LSU as soon as Dexter had told me about his offer.

I'd been wary to send him off to a major city in the south to begin with, the reputation of the state clouding my own judgment and keeping me from actually being as supportive as I could've been. Don't get me wrong, I was damn happy he'd gotten accepted to a college early, regardless of where it was located even if being gay in the south had always sounded like a death sentence to me. One that would end in ostracisation or worse.

The more I saw of Baton Rouge, the more I was beginning to understand why Gage wasn't willing to leave it behind and why Dexter was considering coming here in the first place. The culture was rich, the people were hospitable, and there was a ton of stuff to do outside of campus life.

Outside of the same prejudices we'd find in parts of California, Baton Rouge wasn't abnormally terrible on that scale. Not enough for me to spend the rest of this week trying to convince Dexter to look elsewhere for school options.

"Yeah, I was thinking that." He folded up the map into a neat square to stick into his pocket. "I'm not really that informed on agriculture. But if I ever wanted to go into a program like that, LSU obviously has a good one."

"I'll say." If these gardens were anything to go by, my kid would be opening up his own damn farm by the end of his Bachelor's. "How are you liking having the twins around? They're not giving you too much trouble, are they?"

Dexter shook his head. "They're nice. I like them. It's kind of funny watching them and Gage bicker. I get an up close personal look into what it would've been like if I had a sibling."

I held back a snort.

There were times before Kate and I broke up where we'd talked about having another one. Obviously, that never came into fruition with my cheating and breaking up our marriage, though the idea still entertained itself years after that.

At one point, I'd gotten so desperate after having lost Dexter that I'd walked into a damn donor bank and asked to be matched with someone who was willing to have an open IVF journey that I could step in and help co-parent. I'd been chased off the property soon after, my prayers for another child going unanswered.

During that time, I'd even contemplated calling up Kate and telling her that regardless of how she felt about me, Dexter deserved a sibling. Thankfully, I'd never gotten the courage to do that and had let myself wallow until the pain numbed me.

Those were some of my darker days that I'd take to the grave and tell no one about. Something in the universe had been looking out for me back then, not wanting me to help bring another child into this world when I was already severely fucked up and not dealing with it well.

"Do *you* like them?" he asked.

"Yeah, they're good kids." I used my hand on his back to guide Dexter away from the middle of the boardwalk as a large family moved past us, heading in the opposite direction. "I'm surprised you clicked with them so easily."

"I *am* capable of making friends," he drawled.

Wincing, I said, "That's not what I meant."

Even though that's definitely what I'd been implying.

If Dexter wanted to keep his circle of friends small, then it wasn't really my place to say anything. Despite my initial worries about him when I'd talked to Gage about it, he was clearly capable of befriending whoever he wanted with no signs of the stunted social skills that I'd previously worried about.

"Uh huh," was all he said back, guiding us onto another pathway.

"I'm sorry. I know I'm being overprotective."

Admitting that out loud to anyone other than Gage had me clamming up with self-consciousness. We were supposed to be in the 'mentor/guide' phase of our relationship, according to the parenting books I'd been given by my therapist late last year. Except missing out on all of the milestones with him before this stage had left me trying to overcompensate big time.

Now, I was at that fun stage of uncertainty where every misstep felt astronomical.

"It's fine. You're not half as bad as mom and Dan." He rolled his eyes. "I swear they'd lock me up in a bubble if it was legal."

"That bad, huh?" Not that I couldn't imagine Kate going overboard with her overprotectiveness, either. We were both grabbing at Dexter and yanking him in opposite directions, even with us being newly cordial.

Hearing that his stepfather was similar, though, had me curious. "Do you like him? Dan, I mean."

Dexter shrugged. "He's fine. He can get a bit over the top when he's trying to get his point across. He was pissed when I told mom that I didn't want to go to church anymore two summers ago. He tried taking me to this lecture at another church a few towns over to try and convince me to go again."

"That sounds... a bit much."

"That's how Dan is. He's been that way

since I can remember. I think he still sees me as just mom's kid and not his stepson, which is fine, I guess. I'm not really bothered by it. It only gets annoying when he tries to ground me or force me into doing things that I don't want to do like the church thing. The entire time, I felt so weird because he barely pays attention to me otherwise." Dexter shook his head. "I don't do anything bad. So, I don't know what his deal is."

How complicated.

No wonder Dexter was standoffish with me. Aside from the obvious that he hardly knew me, having some man trying to come in and take over the father role he'd been without for so long must've felt like a slap in the face no matter how I framed it at the time.

Why were any of us surprised when he

dug his heels in to resist the change?

The only consistency he's ever had was his mother.

I wanted to believe that Kate's choice in a husband after me was carefully considered and not an impulsive move in order to fulfill a role that I was no longer available for. No matter how I felt about her replacing me so easily when I'd begged her to let me in.

In the end, Dexter had turned out to be a very thoughtful, smart, and idealistic person that had a bright future ahead of him. None of which I could chalk up to having been born out of my influence. Maybe now for the future, I could take some credit, but for now, this was still all Kate.

Throwing my arm around his shoulders, I brought him against my side to squeeze him. "Listen, you're an incredible person, Dex. Don't let anyone tell you or let you think otherwise. I'm so damn proud of you. Anyone would be lucky to call you their son."

He blinked up at me, his lips parting in surprise. "You... really mean that?"

"Of course I do. I wouldn't be saying it if I didn't."

A small smile tugged at his lips. His gaze darted away from me bashfully while his voice was quiet, barely able to be heard over the breeze picking up through the trees. "Thanks, dad."

"Anytime."

I let my arms slip from him and back down to my sides. His shoulder brushed with mine as a couple of joggers came up from behind us and passed us on either side, their faces red and chests heaving heavily from their workout.

Both of us fell into a peaceful lull of silence. I didn't think I'd ever be able to express to him how grateful I was that he'd asked me to take him on this trip. In just the span of a few short days, I felt closer to him than I had this entire past year.

Dexter letting me into his world inch by inch felt just as rewarding as getting my damn one year sober chip.

"You know," when he finally spoke again, I looked at him. "If I end up going to LSU, you could move here, too. Gage seems pretty happy to have you around."

Wryly, I said, "Trying to set me up?"

He shrugged, though there was that same small smile playing on his lips from earlier. "Aren't you tired of long distance?"

"God. Yes." I sighed. I was tired of a lot

of things that were getting in the way of Gage and I. For one, his weird hot and cold attitude. But I wasn't sure how much of that was from us being forced into close proximity with a full house or something else going on with him. "I don't know if living together is the right move right now, though."

Dexter frowned. "Why not?"

"It's complicated."

He stared at me.

Jesus, who knew my kid would be this invested in my love life. "I think I upset him, but I'm not sure how. So, he's been a little off with me the past few days."

"Huh." Dexter turned back to face the boardwalk. "So, what do you think happened?"

"Kid, if I knew, I would've solved it by now."

He snorted. "All right. True. You guys aren't... breaking up, right?"

Aw, was he worried?

That warmed my heart if that was the case. Going from being terrified of him knowing I was dating someone, to him finding out and trying to give me relationship advice was a one-eighty flip that I never would've predicted but welcomed wholeheartedly.

"No, no. Nothing like that. Sometimes couples go through weird phases. I'm sure we'll be fine once I get him to actually talk to me."

He fell into another contemplative silence, his teeth gnawing on his bottom lip. Sometimes I wished I could reach in there and take a peek at those thoughts that always seemed to be rattling around inside of his head.

XAVIER

"I can ask Asher and Greyson to take me out tonight somewhere. Maybe a local restaurant or something so that you and Gage can have some privacy to talk," he finally suggested.

I threw my arm back around him again, bringing him in so I could press a quick peck to the side of his head. "Hey, no meddling. You just worry about yourself and enjoying your vacation. I don't want you stressing about this. I appreciate you caring, but I swear we're okay. Couples sometimes go through rough patches, it happens. I'm sure you've seen your mom and Dan go through something similar a couple of times."

He grunted at me. "That doesn't count. They preach at each other until one of them gives up and goes to bed for the night."

I held back making a face. "They still make up in the end, though, right?"

"I guess?"

Oh, boy.

Well, it wasn't exactly my place to speculate on my ex-wife's relationship with her husband. As far as I knew, they weren't splitting up anytime soon. "I appreciate you worrying about me."

"Fine. All right. Message received."

"I love you, Dex."

He smiled again, shrugging my arm off of him. "Love you, too, dad."

We pit-stopped at a small pavilion that had a couple of restrooms attached to the back of it. I leaned against the side of the building while Dexter headed around to the bathrooms, giving me the chance to pull out my phone and check my messages.

There was only one from Gage that was him replying to my message from earlier telling him that we'd arrived at the botanical gardens safe and sound. While at face value, there was nothing wrong with what he'd said back, I could tell we were still at the same place we were two days ago.

Since then, he'd seemed to be masking whatever it was that he was feeling off about, causing us both to fall into a weird and stilted rhythm that I absolutely hated.

Maybe Dexter was right—maybe we did need to take tonight to work things out and talk. I hadn't wanted to push him on the subject since, believing that giving him space would end with him coming around to talking to me about it.

But maybe that was simply my way of being a coward. I'd left it all on Gage's shoulders to bring to me without providing the proper space for him to do so. Telling him I'd be around for whenever he felt like opening up wasn't the same thing as bringing the problem to the table and asking him to talk to me about it.

I could plead with him all I wanted about talking to me, and unless he was suddenly feeling no longer clammed up about it, we were going nowhere.

Typing up a text to send to him, I read it over a few times before hitting 'send'.

<<*What time do you get off tonight? I want to take you out. Just you and me.*

His reply was almost instant.

>>*Really?? Where? I get off at six :)*

There was my eager boyfriend. The man loved to be wined and dined regardless of what was going on between us.

<<*I'll look up some local spots. We'll head out around 6:30.*

A sudden scream shook me hard enough to push away from the wall and swing around to the back side of the building where I'd heard it coming from. My phone vibrated with Gage's incoming text right as I shoved it into my pocket.

"Get away from me!" someone shouted again, sounding a hell of a lot like my son.

My heart thumped hard in my chest as I ran to the bathrooms.

CHAPTER TWENTY-ONE

Xavier

SHOVING OPEN THE double swinging door into the men's stalls, I found a man standing at the back of the bathroom with his hand holding open one of the stall doors at the end. His head whipped around the second he heard me enter, his hands immediately coming up to either side of his head.

"I didn't do anything," he said to me.

He was around my age, maybe a little older, with a bald head, and wide-framed glasses that made his head look egg-shaped. He was tall and lanky, with a backpack slung over his one shoulder. His zip-up hoodie was parted funny, almost like he'd haphazardly zipped it in a hurry. The rest of him was dirty, stained with dark spots along his knees and pant cuffs.

"You followed me!" Dexter shouted from somewhere behind him.

"Get away from him," I snapped, marching down the aisle.

The man flattened himself against the wall, his hands still raised in the air while he scooted along to inch toward the door.

Ignoring him, I headed over to Dexter's stall that was still halfway open, finding him curled up against the corner of it and tucked practically behind the toilet. He had his arms wrapped tightly around him while his entire body shook violently.

His eyes were wide and dilated when they snapped to me.

"What the hell happened?" I asked.

"H-he..." With a shaky hand, Dexter pointed to the side of his door. "B... busted the lock."

Grabbing the door again, I looked down to where the simple metal bar that was used to hold the door in place was now hanging on by a single screw, facing the floor instead of horizontal to the door. My heart sank in my stomach, the picture suddenly becoming clearer.

Whipping around to where the man had been standing, I spotted no one else inside of the small bathroom other than us.

Fuck.

"H-He..." Dexter choked out. "He just... I was trying to... go to the bathroom and..."

"You're okay, Dex." Shoving myself into the stall with him was difficult, even with the way he was pressed back against the far wall. I reached out to grab at his arm to try and gently coax him out but he refused to move.

Tears spilled down his cheeks, a loud sob following right after. He was shaking so hard that I was afraid he was actually having a seizure. Pivoting my body to the side, I got the door shoved closed behind me and kept it that way with a hand planted on the top of it.

Reaching across the short distance, I took Dexter by the arm again, but instead of trying to pull him toward me, I ushered him down to the floor instead, letting him cram himself back into his tight corner without the risk of him passing out and falling.

He buried his head into his knees and rocked himself, his sobs barely muffled while they reverberated against the tiled walls around us.

"Dex, you're okay, I'm right here. I know that was scary." I cupped the top of his head with my hand to run my fingers through his hair. "I wouldn't let anything bad happen to you."

When I caught that guy—because when I got this all sorted out I would hunt him down until I was able to wrap my hands around that skinny neck—he was going to wish he never stepped foot on this damn property.

My military training would be pinpoint

focused on making sure that man never walked, let alone tried to peep on another teenager, again.

"How?" he managed to choke out, lifting his face away from his knees just enough to talk. "You—you didn't... you didn't know..."

This was definitely a panic attack, with how hard his breath was coming in and out of him. I'd had very little experience dealing with something like this for a kid, and had even less training on what to do to break someone out of it.

Dexter's face was red from how hard he was crying. Tears continued to leak down his cheeks and pool onto the fabric of his jeans. He was heaving air into his lungs, not quite catching enough of it before another sob took over and forced it all back out again.

"You screamed and I came." I swallowed the bile rising in my throat and tried to keep my voice level as I spoke. "That's all I needed."

"Not last time."

What the fuck?

"What do you mean 'last time'?"

He shook his head, burying it against his knees once more.

My throat clogged up, a wave of nausea hitting me. "Dex, what do you mean 'last time'? What happened?"

The memories of Dexter's almost confession to me late last year hit me like a train, slamming into me with enough force that I had to lean back against the door of the stall to steady myself.

The urge to deny the truth laid out in front of me—to beg for it to not be real— was bringing tears to my eyes. The evidence was too clear to deny, Dexter's panic attack too severe for this to have been a first time thing.

This was the stuff of repeated trauma slapping you across the cheek with a swiftness that shocked you down to your core. The kind that I'd lived with for the past two decades that still stole my breath away at times.

"Who the fuck hurt you, Dexter?"

When he finally lifted his head again, he whispered, "Father Thomas."

My heart shattered to pieces.

Does your mother know?

Those words were what almost came out of my mouth next before I bit my tongue hard enough to hurt. Now was not the time to be asking him questions. Right now, I needed to snap him back into reality before he actually passed out and hurt himself.

Pushing away from the stall door again gave me enough room to lift Dexter up from where he was and slide him over to me. He crumbled against my chest the second I wrapped my arms around him, clinging to me in the same way he had when he was a toddler.

He buried his face against my shoulder and continued to tremble. I rocked him with me, keeping my hand steady against his back to try and ground him while I spoke to him softly like I had when he had nightmares after Kate and I put him to bed as a baby.

This horrible secret he'd been carrying with him this whole time, not able to talk about it as it festered away at his soul, was the worst injustice I'd ever seen.

Who in their right mind would hurt

someone like Dexter?

Take advantage of him in the most sickest and twisted way possible?

I didn't need to know the details to know how bad they were. Dexter wasn't the kind of person to crack easily, not like this. So whatever this Father Thomas had done to him was horrific enough to break him apart.

"Breathe with me, Dex," I said, pulling in a lungful of air.

It took a few tries, but eventually, he was able to suck in enough oxygen to start calming down his nervous system. After a few more deep breathing exercises, he turned to jello in my arms—utterly exhausted from his adrenaline finally crashing.

I hardly felt his weight while throwing one of his arms over my shoulder and hiking him up enough to get one of my arms tucked around his legs, allowing me to stand and get us both up off the floor.

He hardly moved as I readjusted him and carried him out of the bathroom in a half-fireman hold, half-lifted up onto my shoulder. The man from earlier was still nowhere to be found, probably halfway to the parking lot by now.

How long he'd been following my son, I had no clue. We'd been too focused on our conversation to really pay attention to anyone else around us, outside of the occasional need to move out of the way.

It sickened me to think that my son had been targeted, whether abruptly or through a series of carefully planned moves that I hadn't caught on to at all by the predator lurking right out in broad daylight.

What kind of father was I?

I had the kind of military training that would make more people blanch at, and to have something like this slip past my radar?

Fuck.

I was no better than a random man off the street with no training.

The people passing us by on the trail shot me strange looks when I passed them, though none of them seemed to be reaching for their phones to call the authorities, thankfully. An attendant called to me on the way off the trail but I ignored them in favor of heading right for the parking lot where our rental car was waiting for us.

I tucked a sleeping Dexter into the backseat and strapped him in, trying my best not to wake him while I shut the door and headed over to the driver's side. My hands shook taking the wheel and pulling the car out of park, even more so when I glanced back in my mirror to see my sleeping son's face.

How did I not know?

How *could* I have known?

Two warring thoughts in my head that wouldn't leave me alone the entire fifteen minutes it took to get back to Gage's house. Forcing back my own panic with practiced ease helped me get my kid out of the car and behind the safety of a locked front door.

Dexter stirred slightly when I laid him down in bed and pulled the covers over him, mumbling something in his sleep that I couldn't quite catch.

I didn't know how long I stayed with him, sitting on the side of his bed while I stroked his hair as he slept. Not until I heard voices coming from the front of the house that sounded like Gage talking to someone on the phone.

Slipping out of Dexter's room and shutting the door behind me, I found Gage tossing his work duffle bag onto the floor by the door while he bent at the waist to wrestle his shoes off. He jumped when he turned and spotted me standing there, the person who he was talking to continued to rattle on about something—a party?

Oh, his work party.

"Hey, baby." He smiled, and then glanced down at his phone. "Ellie, I'll call you back later."

He cut her off mid-sentence to drop the call and shove his phone back into his pocket. I watched in real time as his expression fell from the 'happy to see me' down to deep concern.

"Hey, what happened? You look white as a ghost."

He grabbed both of my arms to guide me into the living room, apparently realizing before I had—most likely from his training—that I was about to drop. Right as he hovered me over the couch, my legs collapsed out from under me, sending me catapulting onto the soft cushion.

"Xavier?"

I bent forward to curl my hands over my face, doubling over while the nausea was strong enough to bring stars into my vision. My whole world—the entire axis of it—was now completely off kilter. I'd left this morning living a completely different life to the one I came home with.

My baby boy had been hurt and I wasn't there to protect him.

God, the way he'd said *you weren't there last time,* was going to fucking haunt me.

Gage ran a hand down my back a few times, patiently waiting for me to talk.

How in the world was I supposed to get any words out when all I could focus on was the utter terror on my son's face?

Was that the expression Father Thomas had seen when he'd hurt my son?

Was that enough to stop him or was it the green light to keep going?

Fuck.

"I'm gonna be sick."

Gage snapped into action immediately. Both of his arms hooked under mine to yank me up from the couch and drag me down the hallway to the bathroom. We both stumbled inside, the brightness from the hallway our only light source. I sank onto the floor just as Gage lifted up the toilet seat and pushed my head forward to hover over the clean porcelain bowl.

I clung to the rim, coughing up my entire lunch and breakfast. The clenching in my stomach was painful, causing tears to prickle at the corners of my eyes while I held on for dear life.

Gage rubbed my back through bouts of nausea, not at all cringing away from my spitting bile out of my mouth.

My breathing echoed against the walls of the small bathroom, reminding me of the way Dexter's had inside of that tiny stall.

"Dexter okay?" Gage asked, once it seemed that there was nothing left in my stomach to throw up.

I shook my head, squeezing my eyes shut. "He told me what happened."

His hand froze on my back.

Both of us had gone back and forth on what Dexter had told me last year, or rather what he *didn't* tell me, on what we thought was possibly going on with him. *Neither* of us had ever guessed anything remotely close to this mess.

"The fucking priest." My voice was gravely and my throat burned as I spoke. "At that fucking church she was taking him to."

"Fuck," Gage breathed out. "Where is he?"

"Sleeping."

Peeling my eyes back open, I reached across the way to snag a few squares of toilet paper to wipe my mouth with before tossing it into the bowl and flushing the whole thing. Pitching backward, I settled myself back against the cool tile of the floor, letting my body relax into it.

I had a sense of déjà vu as Gage hovered over me as I lay there, panting, his silhouette shrouded from the light coming from the hallway.

"Oh, honey..."

He gently swiped his fingers under my eyes and belatedly, I realized I was crying.

"I wasn't there..." I said.

The guilt crushed me—more than it had when he'd told me how I was a stranger to him an entire year ago. This was something entirely different, the kind of guilt that I'd felt being the only survivor among my troop and now had to grapple with living when they didn't.

How could I be there for Dexter when I

hadn't been at his most vulnerable moment?

How could I call myself *a father?*

"You didn't know," Gage soothed.

"I should've been there," I whispered back.

He shook his head at me. "You didn't know what you didn't know, baby. It's not your fault or anyone else's other than that bastard who hurt him."

More tears stung my eyes. "I failed him."

"Baby…"

I stared up at the ceiling, tracing the weird shadows with my gaze.

What now?

How did I go from here?

It wasn't like I could go to that church and find the bastard and kill him. Getting myself thrown in jail was the last thing

Dexter needed. He needed me to be there to protect him, something that I couldn't do locked behind bars for the next twenty-five years.

What he needed was to be home with familiarity. To have the comforts of what he knew, not out here trying to put on a brave face and forced to be around people he really didn't know while we toured a random city for the next few days before Christmas.

How could I, in good conscience, keep him away from all of that when this was the time he needed it most?

"I think... I going to take him home," I said.

Gage's voice was quiet as he said, "Do what you need to do."

CHAPTER TWENTY-TWO

Gage

MY HEART HURT for both Xavier and Dexter.

After getting him up off the floor of the bathroom, I'd convinced him to let me cook something for the both of them before they headed off for an early bedtime. Whipping together something both comforting and *good* was tough, but I'd managed to make a homemade classic in the form of goulash.

By the time I'd gotten the food on Xavier's plate, he'd already booked two plane tickets back to California for first thing in the morning. While it wasn't my place to tell him how to handle a situation like this, I was sad to see him and Dexter leaving so abruptly.

I could understand from a parent's perspective on wanting to take your kid back to the familiar comforts that they were used to in order to ground them back down into reality, but at the same time, I was also of the mindset that sometimes distracting yourself until you were ready to face your demons was the best medicine.

Xavier was always going to be overly protective of Dexter, no matter what his age. I found that admirable, even as sad as I was at the time. Putting his child first above all else was the kind of thing he'd only dreamed of a year ago when he'd still been addicted to the bottle.

Having *anyone* take priority over that was impressive in and of itself, no matter how you lookcd at it.

So really, who was I to judge in the grand scheme of things?

"Mmm, something smells tasty."

Turning to the sound of the voice, I spotted Asher wandering into the kitchen, his shoes still on from coming in. Normally, I'd yell at him to take them off but at this point, I was feeling exhausted myself.

Watching Xavier go through all of that and feeling the mental toll of him showing me his booked plane tickets had me wanting to crawl into bed for the next few days and only to come out to pee.

The other downside was tonight Xavier was sleeping in Dexter's room just in case he woke up with a night terror.

"Leftovers are in the fridge," I said, setting the pot down into the sink to soak it.

"Red sauce? Wow, someone was feeling fancy." Asher popped open the door to the fridge, fishing out one of the containers I'd used to store his portion. "What's the occasion?"

"Nothing. Just wanted to make something for Xavier and Dexter."

"Oh, they're here? I didn't even see them." He tossed the container into the microwave and jabbed the buttons on the front of it after shutting the door. "They have a long day at the botanical garden?"

Sighing, I said, "Something like that.

They're taking an early night since they need to catch a plane in the morning."

Asher turned to me with a frown. "Wait, I thought they were staying the rest of the week?"

Turning back to the sink to occupy myself, I said, "Something came up."

Asher was quiet while his food was cooking, giving me time to turn on the sink and rinse out one of the pans I'd used to cook the ground meat in. Normally, I'd be bragging to the high heavens that I'd successfully cooked a meal without having to rely on a store bought base.

Expressing anything remotely close to joy felt wrong right now, though. My stomach was still churning with what Xavier had told me. He didn't have much info about what exactly the priest had done to poor Dexter, but honestly, there wasn't really a reason to force the kid into spilling more details.

It was pretty obvious what happened—given his reaction and the answers to a few of Xavier's questions.

Not to mention that creep who was trying to peep on him got away with not one repercussion for what he was trying to do. Honestly, I had half a mind to call up some of my buddies in the police force and tell them to check the cameras.

Having a guy like that wandering a public space that usually had a lot of kids running around was dangerous.

"So... what happened?" Asher asked just as the microwave went off.

"It's not really my business to say."

He shut the door after pulling the container out, the entire thing ghosting the air with water vapors. "You guys didn't get into a fight or anything, right?"

I shook my head. "Nothing like that. Something... uh, happened to Dexter."

Asher looked concerned at that. "He okay?"

How was I supposed to answer that?

No, not exactly?

Or, yes, hopefully, he would be eventually?

Ugh, this is why I wished Xavier was at least staying up for a little while with me. My brothers could be such damn nosey twits, which made it hard for me to keep things to myself.

I wasn't about to go around spilling all of the details that Xavier had told me about Dexter's situation—he'd told all of that to me in confidence, and regardless of what tactics my brother used to try and weasel the info out of me, I wasn't cracking.

However, straight up lying to my brother when I knew the truth about Dexter's condition felt wrong. I wasn't one to hide things from them, even if it was the brutal honest truth. The world was never going to sugar coat things for you as soon as you stepped into it as a fresh adult.

So why should I?

That would simply be setting my brothers up for failure in a system that was already wildly unbalanced.

"He's... okay, I think. He had something happen to him at the botanical garden. So, his dad is taking him home tomorrow to be with his family."

"That doesn't sound good." Asher fished a fork out of the drawer next to him to stir his goulash around. "What time are they leaving? I can get Grey up in the morning so we can say goodbye."

I smiled a little. "That's really sweet but I think they're trying to get out of here as fast as possible. I can send them a text from all of us once they're back home."

He continued to stir his food around in the container, both of his brows pulled together. "I'm not really liking the sound of all of this. Are they both really okay?"

"Some guy tried to hurt Dexter today." That was as much info as I was giving him. Even *that* I wasn't sure if it was too much.

"Hurt, as in..." Asher fished.

I shook my head at him, turning back to the dishes in the sink. He sighed at me but didn't push it further, thankfully. Out of the two of them, Asher was always good at knowing when to quit.

"Where's your brother?" I asked.

"Out with someone."

"A date?" I glanced over at him.

"Who knows. He says 'friend', so that could mean anyone."

Too true.

If there was one thing Greyson had going for him, it was his gaggle of 'friends' that were actually people throwing themselves at him. He was a good-looking kid, so I could understand the multiple crushes he had accumulated over the years. Couple that with the whole military thing and... well, no wonder he was out on his third day home.

"None for you?" I asked.

He grunted at me, stabbing down into the pieces of noodle and ground beef like he was trying to thatch a bundle of hay.

"Come on, you can't tell me you haven't had anyone hitting you up after finding out you're home." I chuckled.

"Yeah, well. No, I don't."

Okay, that was a total surprise.

Aside from them both being identical, they were both charming to a fault, which had gotten them in and out of trouble many a times during high school. Having to go down to that damn campus every other week had been a true testament to my patience as a caretaker and one that I'd welcomed in dropping the proverbial hat as soon as they graduated.

If Greyson was getting plenty of action, then by default, Asher would be, too. At least patterns from their past suggested as much.

Unless...

"Someone else entertaining you?" I

guessed.

Asher's eyes widened briefly before he focused back on shoving a fork full of food into his mouth.

Bingo.

"Tell me."

So that I can rag on you for it.

As brotherly payback and all, seeing as how when I'd finally told them about Gage, they hadn't dropped teasing me about it for weeks. While endearing that they were all for me finally finding someone I clicked with, after about the fourth week, I'd been over it.

"Tell you what? I've got nothing." His tone was a little more defensive than usual.

"Asher Torres, you tell me who's keeping you preoccupied."

He scoffed. "No one, okay? Maybe I

want to be single and focus on my work at the ranch."

The ranch...

Actually, wasn't Greyson saying something about his boss a while back?

Some handsome guy that had Asher dragging himself out of bed *willingly* before the sun rose?

I was positive I wasn't imagining that.

"Not your boss at the ranch?"

He choked on his food hard enough to toss the container onto the counter and pound his fist against his chest a few times. I doubled it up by slapping him on the back, finally getting the noodle loose from his throat so he could breathe again.

"*Fuck*," he muttered.

"Wow, so was that a yes?"

He slammed his elbow into my ribs, causing me to yelp and shuffle away.

"Rude," I said, grabbing my dishtowel to snap it in his direction. "You know, I can't be a supportive brother if you don't tell me things."

"There's nothing to tell, I'm serious. My boss is..."

I waited while he trailed off, sure he was going to finish his thought. All he actually did, though, was to sigh and roll his eyes while giving his goulash a glare that could rival my own.

"He's what, Ash?"

"Just. Ugh, it's hard to explain." Waving a hand in the air, he snatched his food back off the counter and quickly finished it off.

I grabbed the empty container from him to dunk under the water in the sink. Well, if he wasn't going to tell me anything, I was just going to have to bother Greyson about it. *One* of them was going to have to let me in.

Besides, this was all a nice distraction from the shit with Xavier and Dexter. Teasing my brothers over their love lives was a much simpler path than trying to sort through my tangled emotions regarding a teenage boy who was close to my own two brother's ages being assaulted by someone that he was supposed to be able to trust.

That kind of shit sent me down into a spiral that I didn't want to be dealing with. This world was already scary enough with the drugs, gang violence, corrupt government, and shitty healthcare. Adding predators on top of that was a layer of 'fucked up' that I really didn't want to be thinking about.

Then again, was that a kind of

privilege I was experiencing that Dexter didn't have the luxury of?

My heart broke for him, absolutely. How this world could be so dark, I'd never know.

I held back another sigh, scrubbing at the leftover container with a kind of rigorousness that had my hands hurting. Whatever Xavier, and by default Dexter, needed in the future to help this transition easier on them, I would one hundred percent be there to help provide it.

Forget all of the bullshit surrounding my insecurities. That could all wait until Xavier got settled down into a good place again. And Dexter, too.

If they ever wanted to come back before the school year ended for a do-over of this turned-shitty vacation, my place had an open door and a warm bed waiting for them. No questions asked.

Hell, I'd pay for the goddamn plane tickets the minute Xavier called me to ask if it was all right to crash here again.

Hopefully, I wouldn't be kept waiting for long. Because while I wanted Xavier to spend time with his family during this difficult situation, I also missed him, too. As selfish as that was.

"Gage?" Asher hovered over my shoulder. "I think that thing is clean."

"Oh shit." Pulling it out of the water, the scrapper side of my poor sponge was mangled by how hard I'd been rubbing it against the lip of the container, cutting it up and shredding it into pieces that were now floating on the water's surface.

"You good?" Asher asked.

"Yeah, just got caught up in my

thoughts."

Like fucking usual.

He threw an arm around my shoulders, jostling me slightly to pull me close to him. "Hey, I know you're sad about your boytoy leaving before the party, but at least you have me and Grey."

Smiling, I set the container down and tossed the sponge onto the side of the sink. "Of course. I'm not complaining one bit. You two surprising me was the best Christmas gift you could've ever gotten me."

He grinned. "Yeah? Just wait until your *real* gift."

The shimmering mischief in his eyes told me *exactly* what I needed to know about the goddamn mystery box he and his brother had teased me with their first day back in the state. I supposed it would be a tradition to prank me after having been gone for so long.

I only hoped that it wasn't another whipped cream pie this time around.

That shit was surprisingly hard to get out of your clothes.

"Uh huh." Nudging him, I slipped out from under his arm to grab the towel hanging off the stove. "Listen, you two need to behave a little bit at the party. Some of my coworkers are a little on the reserved side."

"What about Quinn? He seemed totally cool with Grey and I."

Ugh, of course you think that.

I'd seldom brought the twins around the station when they were kids—mostly because emergencies could rarely ever be predicted and having them be in the way of some kind of chaotic go-go-go was a scene out of my worst nightmare.

Sure, they'd *probably* be fine, but there was always the possibility that they *wouldn't* be. And I just couldn't be taking that lightly. As they'd gotten older, they'd stopped by a little more frequently, but not enough to really know the newbies we'd gotten in recently.

Which tended to be a good thing sometimes.

"Quinn... will be preoccupied at the party." Hopefully.

Knowing Quinn, though, both he and Jase would be getting roped into Asher and Greyson's schemes in no time. Zander, too, probably.

Hopefully, Ellie didn't put me on extra cleaning duty if the twins made a mess of the place.

"Well, either way, I'm excited to see all your coworkers. Greyson, too."

That really warmed my heart, even if I knew Asher was most likely planning something ridiculous. "I'm glad. Why don't you go change and we can grab a movie on the couch while we wait up for your brother to come back with his tales of his nightly escapades."

Asher flashed me a grin. "Hell yeah, count me in."

CHAPTER TWENTY-THREE

Xavier

PULLING INTO THE driveway to Kate's house, I killed the ignition and let the car rattle to a cool with Dexter and me still sitting inside of the cab. Both of us had barely talked the entire trip back to California, outside of the occasional check-ins after getting through TSA and then on and off the plane.

While there was a lot left unsaid

between us, I was sure we both agreed that the exhaustion from this impromptu trip had won out over that entirely. Dexter wasn't exactly surprised when I woke him up early this morning with both of our bags packed and an outfit laid out for him.

Nor was he taken aback when Gage met us at the door to bid us a soft, heartfelt goodbye that left tears in my eyes when we climbed into the rental car and jetted off for the airport.

Yesterday seemed like an entire lifetime ago compared to now. Idling in Kate's driveway had somehow taken me off autopilot, slowly pulling me back into my consciousness and reality. The gravity of 'now what' weighed on me more than I'd really anticipated.

There were no rule books that came

with dealing with situations like this one. No proper protocol was discussed in Parenting 101 when you first met your baby in the hospital and all of the nurses and doctors came around to congratulate you on your new bundle of joy.

Why could this world be so dark and cruel and why were those that perpetrated against the laws of nature allowed to still walk freely among us with seemingly no consequences?

I was so lost, so goddamn angry.

"Just tell me one thing, Dex…" My voice was soft as I spoke. "And I won't ask you anything else about this until you're ready to talk."

His face was obscured by his hood pulled up over his head, intentionally left like that throughout our entire journey home save for the one time TSA had asked him to pull it down to confirm his identity.

When he slowly turned away from looking out the windshield, his eyes were glazed over from lack of sleep and the rough ride we'd had coming home from being crammed back in economy.

"Does mom know?" I asked.

His lips thinned into a small frown. My heart sank at the way his gaze moved away from mine, his eyes downcast into his lap where he fiddled with his hands.

"A little."

That's all I needed to know.

I reached over to put a hand on his shoulder, giving him a reassuring squeeze and a silent 'thank you' for being honest with me.

None of this was easy to talk about at all, and what little info he'd given me so far was enough to paint the picture he was trying to tell me without actually having to relive the trauma of recounting the entire situation.

I appreciated anything at this point.

But now I had an even bigger problem—my ex-wife and her not informing me about this. If she found out recently, that was one thing, but there was a deep twisting in my gut telling me otherwise.

Kate wasn't one to bring me in on anything when it came to Dexter without humiliating me first into begging on my hands and knees for the damn crumbs she decided to bless me with whenever she felt like it.

I didn't want to be bitter toward her, not when deep down in my heart, I knew that whatever Kate's choices were, they were made in good faith to keep Dexter safe even when I didn't agree with them.

But this was so much different.

This was not her putting him into a private Catholic school against my wishes, or forcing him into some sports club when he obviously wanted to get onto the debate team. This wasn't her bringing him to church every Sunday to sit in some goddamn pew for two hours while praying to a God that I was pretty sure our kid didn't even believe in.

The second she found out about any of this, she should've been showing up on my doorstep demanding to talk to me. Because that's sure as fuck what I was about to do right now.

Climbing out of the car, I let the door slam shut behind me and grabbed the handle of the one behind me to fish

Dexter's bag out. He got out after me a moment later, slowly sliding off of his seat until his feet finally hit the pavement.

His body was hunched in on itself while he grabbed onto one of the strings coming down from his hoodie. Coming around the other side of my car, I watched him hover next to his door for a long moment, staring at the front door that was still closed and the light above it still on from the night before.

"I'll let them know you're tired so they leave you alone to sleep," I said, trying to offer him what I hoped was a reassuring smile.

His frown only deepened, though, his body still unmoving.

This horrible situation, however long it had been going on for Dexter, only seemed to encourage his reserved nature.

Not that I could really blame him for wanting to shut himself off from the rest of the world at this point.

What good was any of it to him when all it seemed to throw at him was fucking nightmares?

"I'm sorry, dad."

Wait, what the fuck?

"Dex, no, you have nothing to be sorry for! None of this is your fault."

"But we cut the trip short because I—"

"Son, no. No."

I waved a hand at him, holding my arm up to beckon him over until he finally peeled himself away from the side of my car to shuffle over to me. His body practically sagged into mine when he reached me, allowing me to wrap a tight arm around him as I guided him up to the front steps leading into the house.

XAVIER

I hadn't bothered to call Kate ahead of time about any of this, mainly out of pure avoidance. There was no doubt in my mind that as soon as I called or even texted her that we were coming home earlier than she'd anticipated, I would've had a slew of calls and texts popping up on my notification bar the second we landed.

Call me selfish but I really wasn't in the mood to be dealing with any of that.

Even now, standing there as I rang the doorbell, I felt a headache coming on.

After a minute of us waiting, the lock on the other side of the door clicked as it was shoved back from the dead bolt, the door opening a moment later. A man, tall, with glasses and a large forehead, stood in front of the glass storm door with a confused expression on his face.

Both of us stepped back so he could push the door open. "Dexter? I thought you were coming home later this week?"

"Dan, right?" I shoved a hand in the gap separating the door from the frame. "I'm Xavier. It's nice to meet you."

He glanced down at my hand with very obvious disdain; the wrinkles forming on his forehead were prominent while his face pinched into a sour look. I held my hand there, plastering a pleasant smile on my face when he finally looked up at me again.

When he slowly took my hand, I squeezed his back, giving it a hard shake. "We had some things come up on the trip. I've got Dex's bag if you want to take it."

Ripping my hand away from his, I used it to push the storm door open further while wiggling the strap of Dexter's bag off my shoulder and passed it between us. Dan's eyes widened and quickly, he took the bag in his arms.

While he was momentarily distracted with that, I nodded to Dexter while continuing to hold the door open. Taking my hint, he ducked under my arm to head inside, disappearing beyond the foyer and hopefully, up to his room where he could lock himself in for the rest of the morning to decompress.

I was damn worried about my kid but I also knew that it was important to give yourself the time to come down from the spike in stress hormones. Fuck, I knew I'd needed plenty of that when I was discharged.

"Is there a reason you brought him back so early?" Dan asked.

While he didn't exactly sound annoyed,

he certainly didn't look too happy.

Was that from the lack of planning on our end, not communicating, or something else?

Such as him not wanting my kid around in general.

I wanted to believe the best in this man, having stepped up where I couldn't, in raising Dexter, no matter what my pride and ego said about some other man raising my son. Yet, I also knew the statistics of men treating their step kids like pariahs due to that very reason.

Would Kate bring a man like that around to help raise Dexter?

I certainly hoped not.

"Kate around?" I asked instead of answering him, leaning around him to look deeper into the house.

He huffed at me, sliding the bag down

to the floor while saying, "Look, I don't know what your game is, but—"

"Dan?" Kate called. "Did I just see Dexter going upstairs?"

Before either of us could answer her, she appeared in the doorway looking shocked to see me. Her dirty blonde hair was wrapped up in a tight ponytail, the long lengths hanging down behind her. Even though it was early in the morning, she had her makeup down and a nice outfit on.

The only thing that was out of place was her slightly white-dusted hands. Presumably from some kind of bread dough she was most likely making for church dinner this coming Sunday.

"Xavier..." she breathed out.

I grabbed the door to yank it completely open. "I need to talk to you."

"I think it's best if you leave," Dan said, fixing me with a glare.

I ignored him, staring my ex-wife down. "It's about Dex. You know I wouldn't be showing up here like this if it wasn't important."

Her expression faltered. Even though she clearly wanted to fight me—most likely to tell me to get the fuck off her property—she knew I was right. I wasn't the kind of jealous ex to show up and demand for her to take me back or something as equally ridiculous.

We took our shit with Dexter seriously. There was no such thing as 'needlessly bothering each other' over trivial matters in order to annoy each other to death. Thankfully, that was the one mature thing we both mutually agreed on long ago.

"Kate," Dan said, a little panicked when she stepped out onto the landing.

"I'll be just a second," she said, swinging the storm door closed behind her.

Dan watched us through the glass, wearing a clearly dissatisfied frown.

Not wanting an audience to this—because who knew if Dan was even aware of this situation—I led Kate down to my car and parked us right around the side of it, facing away from the door. I doubted her new husband could read lips, but on the off chance, I was taking every precaution.

"What happened? Why did you bring him home so early?" She crossed her arms. "Don't tell me you got sick of him over having him for just a weekend."

I ignored the jab. "Dexter told me

about Father Thomas."

Instantly, her face went white.

"When were you going to tell me?" I asked. "Better yet. When did you find out?"

Her arms slowly dropped from her chest while she swallowed audibly.

It hurt more to know that she kept this from me than her questioning the integrity of my parenting before allowing me to take my own kid across state lines for a weekend.

"He... he told you..." she whispered.

"Yes, Kate. I know it may blow your mind to realize that my son *actually* tells me things, but yeah, he told me. When the fuck were you going to tell me and when did *you* find out?"

She fumbled over her words. "Last summer... he— I was having a really hard time taking him to church because he was refusing to go. It was out of the blue, and...” To her credit, she looked like she felt incredibly guilty. “I’m sorry.”

So, around the time he said he’d stopped going to church with her. “Is that when it happened?”

“I-I think so... He didn’t want to talk about it.”

Yeah, no shit.

“Did you report it? What the fuck happened with the priest?”

“Of course I did!” she spat out. “What kind of mother do you take me for?”

“One that doesn’t tell the father jack-shit.” All right, it was a low blow. Sue me. I was too angry with her, with the fucking priest—with the rest of the goddamn world—to care right now.

She flinched. “What, so I was supposed

to call you up and say to you, 'hey, long time no talk. Just to let you know, our son was molested today!'. Is that what you wanted, Xavier?"

"Yes!" I exploded. "What the fuck is wrong with you, Kate?"

"I was *protecting him*—"

"You brought him there! To that fucking church! I told you I didn't want him raised in that shit, and you did it anyway. You handed him over to a fucking predator!"

Her eyes grew watery, looking as though I'd just struck her with my own hand across her cheek. I wanted to feel bad at her stumbling back from me, shocked to hear something so hateful spilling out of my mouth.

The truth of the matter was that I really *didn't* care. Not when I'd been lied to and misinformed about a situation that definitely was supposed to involve both parents in making a decision on what was best for our child.

I should've been there when the police report was filed and when my son had to recount the entire goddamn thing to a room full of strangers with badges. Or afterward, when I was sure he was feeling so raw and exposed it was a wonder he didn't walk right out into the middle of traffic.

"If you tell me Dan fucking knew before I did, I'm going to lose it," I gritted through my teeth.

"He's my *husband*, Xavier. I wasn't going to lie to him about what was going on."

"No, just lie to the father of your child, instead." I tightened my hands into fists.

I forced myself to step away from her before I yelled something even worse at her; my adrenaline was spiking so high that my vision was beginning to tunnel. This was the same kind of intense aggression I felt whenever I was thrown into combat.

A kill-or-be-killed type situation that was slowly morphing into murderous intent. Wherever that priest was, he better count his fucking days because I was coming for him. No matter what jail cell he was rotting inside. I'd pay him a little visit.

"Xavier," Kate choked out. "Stop. Okay? It's done and over with."

"Where is he? Which jail?"

When I turned to her, she was shaking her head. "He's not—"

I ripped open the door to my car before

she even got the sentence out. My thoughts were thundering around me—repeating what an utter failure the justice system really was. Of course the priest walked. Of course they probably transferred him to another parish. Of course my son would never receive any justice.

At that point, I didn't care if I went to jail. At least my son wouldn't have to constantly be afraid and looking over his shoulder.

Kate raced over to me, grabbing the handle from the outside before I could pull it open. She was screaming something at me while I turned the key that I'd left in the ignition, letting the car roar to life.

"Stop!" She grabbed a hold of the front of my shirt, practically throwing herself over my lap to stop me from grabbing at the gearshift. "He's dead! He died!"

My body froze.

"He's dead, Xavier!" she kept repeating. "He killed himself. Please, get out of the car!"

Her nails dug into my arm, using that infamous mom-strength that all women seemed to possess at the most crucial of times, in order to yank me out of the car. I faltered, pitched sideways and crashed onto the driveway, crushing my shoulder in the process.

The sharp and sudden pain was enough to temporarily break me from whatever tunnel vision and hair-brained plan I'd had in going up to Kate's church in order to bust down the doors and drag whatever white-collared fool I could get my hands on to interrogate.

Kate's sobs were what brought me back to reality, along with her nails biting into my skin still.

"I'm sorry," she kept repeating. "I knew you'd go to jail. I'm sorry."

Behind her, Dan hovered just a few feet from where we were, clearly lost on what to do. He'd probably sprinted out as soon as he'd seen her trying to yank me out of the car. Or who knows, maybe it was when we'd begun yelling at each other about our shared responsibility in failing to protect our only child in all of this.

"When," I croaked.

Reading my cryptic question for what it was, she answered, "Right after he was arrested. He hung himself in his cell."

"Coward," I spat out, while pushing myself up from the driveway.

My shoulder screamed from me rotating it a few times to check to make sure I hadn't blown it out of the socket. Outside of the dizzying pain, it would be fine with an ice pack and a few Tylenol.

"He needed you here." Kate sniffled. "Not in a jail cell."

Much the same mantra I'd told myself yesterday after finding out. How funny the way things changed in the blink of an eye.

"You never told me," I said.

"I was going to. Eventually."

I shook my head.

While I wanted to believe her, I didn't know how true that really was when everything finally boiled down to it. Perhaps Kate had the intention to do so back when it first happened, letting the dust settle long enough with the case before bringing it to me because of her genuine—and now proven—fear that I'd do something irrational.

But there wasn't any excuse now that it was almost an entire year later since the actual incident.

"Don't blame her," Dan was saying. "It's not her fault."

"Shut up, Dan," I snapped. I really wasn't in the mood for the fucking peanut gallery to be weighing in on this. "Your fucking church. I'm blaming whoever the fuck I want."

He had no rebuttal to that. Thankfully.

If he opened his mouth again, I really was going to end up taking out all of my aggression on him. Which wasn't going to fair well with asking Kate to let me see Dexter again. In her eyes, I was already on thin ice from the drinking and being out of Dexter's life.

Which... now I supposed the odds were even.

"You're not bringing him back to that fucking church," I said, slowly standing. "Or any of them."

She shook her head, looking up at me. "I haven't, I swear."

For the roles to reverse like this so suddenly was jarring. Now *I* was on the side of the disappointed parent looking down at the fuck-up that caused out son harm and pain.

Perfect Kate was no longer so perfect.

Letting out a long sigh, I let my anger fade into numbness. At this point, there was nothing that could be done. No matter how much I yelled and screamed at Kate over it, she couldn't wave a wand and go back in time to fix any of it.

That ship had come and gone along

with the priest who was, hopefully, now rotting in a hell I no longer believed in but could for this occasion.

At least Dexter was safe from him.

Dan moved closer to us in order to pick Kate up off the driveway. She was still staring at me with those big doe-eyes of hers that I'd gotten so used to seeing during our first few years of marriage. She'd looked to me to be her leader when I'd had no clue what the hell I was doing. She'd put her trust in me in more ways that I probably deserved at the time.

And now here we were, standing face-to-face while we were both lost.

I didn't want to hate her, or blame her, despite my anger. Eventually, I'd probably forgive her, even though for now, that seemed like a very distant wish.

Whatever happened at this point and

moving forward, we needed to do it together. No more of this bullshit with us fighting for control over the other. Clearly that wasn't working for either of us.

"Kate."

Her uncertain stare was all I got in return.

"I need you, going forward, to meet me halfway. We can't keep doing this. I'm tired of being left out of things that are important. I get that I wasn't the best dad around the past decade, but I'm here now. We both fucked up. I need you to stop holding my past over my head, just like I'm choosing not to do so with you right now."

She swallowed visibly.

I held my hand out to her. "We're going to *actually* co-parent from here on out."

Slowly, she placed her hand in mine,

shaking it. "Okay. No more hatchet."

"No more hatchet," I agreed, squeezing her hand.

CHAPTER TWENTY-FOUR

Xavier

"HOW'RE YOU HOLDING up?" Gage asked.

Shifting the ice pack resting on my forehead toward the crown of my head was the only thing that was relieving the pressure from this god awful migraine that had cropped up the second I'd climbed into my car and left Kate's house.

As soon as I'd gotten home, I crawled

into bed with my ice pack and my phone, determined to shut out the rest of the world for the foreseeable future.

While I was glad Kate and I had come to some sort of understanding and agreement between us, I was damn exhausted—both physically and emotionally. Much more so the latter part.

"I'll survive," I finally answered.

Probably not the answer he was looking for, but that's all I could manage to give for now. My brain was too mushed from everything that had happened within the past twenty-four hours. I desperately wanted to pass out and go to sleep but unfortunately my body seemed determined to keep me awake regardless of how fried I felt.

"Too bad I can't give you one of my sleeping pills," Gage mumbled. "I knew I should've slipped one in your bag before you left."

I smiled a little. "As much as I love that you think of me, I'm glad you didn't. I really wasn't in the mood to spend the entire day in TSA jail trying to explain a mystery pill."

"Okay, you have a point."

As soon as I'd crawled into bed, I'd called Gage, not caring if he was busy with work or still sleeping. I'd needed to hear the sound of my boyfriend's voice, even if it lulled me to sleep. Call me childish or clingy, I didn't care.

He had a knack for calming my nervous system down even without the offer of drugs.

"I miss you," I sighed.

"I miss you, too." His voice sounded somber.

While neither of us could've predicted our planned fun-filled week to come crashing down around us, I was glad that no matter what, Gage always took things in stride. He never once made me feel bad about leaving or whined to try and convince me to not follow my gut in bringing Dexter home.

"You and the twins doing okay?"

"Yeah. Asher finally came home last night around two. He was so vague in what he was doing that I felt like some crazy disgraced detective trying to suss out clues as to where he was and with who all night. Of course, Grey was no help."

I huffed out a laugh. "You're such a helicopter mom."

"Ugh, don't remind me."

Despite my teasing, that was one of the

things I loved about him. He showed his care through his overabundance of worry and love—a man with his heart stitched onto his sleeve.

"I love you, Gage."

I could hear the smile in his voice as he said, "I love you, too. Get some sleep, okay? Call me when you get up. I'll have my phone on me."

I breathed out slowly as my body finally started to relax. Almost like it'd been seeking permission to give in and finally rest like I'd be dying to since getting on a plane early this morning.

Listening to the sounds of Gage on the other end of the phone, my body finally fell limp and I slowly drifted off into a dreamless sleep.

CHAPTER TWENTY-FIVE

Xavier

WAKING UP SOME hours later, my body felt less like it'd been run over by a truck and more like I had a hangover from a night of partying—way more manageable in my opinion.

Rolling to sit up, my ice pack, now warm to the touch, slid from my forehead and slapped down into my lap. The room was dark, thanks to my blackout curtains that I'd been smart enough to draw over the windows before crawling into bed.

My phone was somewhere buried under my covers and most likely had a message from Gage waiting for me that I'd answer as soon as I had some food in me.

After blinking the sleep from my eyes, I shoved the covers off of me to roll out of bed. The clock on the nightstand read six-thirty on the dot, which meant I slept almost a full ten hours without waking up once.

As impressive as that was, my body was definitely feeling it given the stiffness in my bones from not moving at all while I'd been passed out. Clearly I'd needed it, though.

Despite the still lingering headache, I did feel better. More clear headed. More in control of my emotions. Less likely to snap and go on a murderous rampage.

That last one might still be up for debate.

Heading into my bathroom, I took a quick shower and freshened up before going back into my room to retrieve my phone. Sure enough, there was a message from Gage wishing me a good sleep with a few emojis accompanying it.

To my surprise, directly under that was one from Dexter that simply read: *'Thank you, dad. I love you'.*

"Ugh." I slapped my hand over my heart while my body pitched forward, overwhelmed with both love and guilt that seemed to want to battle in trying to be at the forefront of whatever my emotions were trying to decide on how I felt.

Even though I knew in the back of my mind that Dexter didn't hate me, a message like this was still a nice confirmation.

I hoped he didn't regret telling me anything. I hoped that from now on, we could turn over a new leaf and start fresh—no more skeletons hidden in the closet.

Typing out a heartfelt reply back to him, I sent it on its way before tossing my phone back onto my bed and grabbing a fresh set of clothes to change into for the evening.

I'd give him the rest of the week to be by himself and then invite him over for dinner and a movie or something. With Christmas right around the corner, there was no sense in overwhelming him with a bunch of activities and running around the city trying to fill the awkward void left by him opening up to me.

XAVIER

Starting small after having gone through some major turmoil was probably best, even if he didn't blame me for it. The last thing I wanted was for Dexter to feel like some kind of freak around me now that I knew his secret. That was a common thing for people to feel when opening up about trauma, yet I didn't want that to happen regardless of the circumstances.

I'd been treated like a damn pariah after being forced out of the closet and outed to everyone around me. So, like hell I was going to let my kid have to go through something similar.

Since Kate and I were agreeing to work together now, I'd have to bring up getting Dexter into some form of counseling before he was off to college in a few months. It wasn't good for him to fester on these horrible memories by himself. He needed an expert to help him work through everything to untangle the mess that had been done to him by someone he should've been able to trust.

No wonder he'd kept everyone at arm's length.

Shaking my head, I made my way across my house to the kitchen. I was suddenly starving, having only eaten a small box of raisins on the plane ride over here that had tasted barely edible. Now that I was back on solid ground, I wanted something that was actually real food.

Passing by the police scanner I kept hooked up to the outlet in my kitchen, I flicked it on to listen to the tones while grabbing a box of pasta out of the pantry. This was the kind of familiarity that grounded me. The only thing missing was my boyfriend crowding up the small space while pretending he knew how to heat a can of red sauce on the stove.

Just as I was setting a pot on the stove to bring it to a boil, the radio went off again with another set of tones, followed by an automated message that said: *"All units and medical personnel, please respond to eight-five-five River Street, Sacramento County."*

I whipped around. That was my street.

Jogging toward my front door, I ripped it open and stepped out onto my porch, facing east to where eight fifty-five was located only five houses down from mine. Black plumes of smoke clouded the sky, billowing up at a fast rate that meant the building that was caught on fire was burning *fast.*

"Fuck."

Of course I didn't have any of my gear with me, but with no sounds of sirens nearby and no flashing lights on the street right outside of the residence, I was going to wager that the next unit on scene wouldn't be there for another two minutes.

Which in the event of a fire, meant life or death.

Sprinting to my closet, I threw on the best thick clothing I had while shoving my feet into a pair of the only thick-soled boots in my closet. Grabbing another shirt off of a hanger, I used it to wrap around the lower half of my face in a makeshift mask. It'd barely help but until the trucks arrived, there wasn't much else I could do.

Heading back to the front of my house, I found my spare axe sitting against the wall in the hall closet where I'd tucked it into the corner for emergencies.

The weight of it was comfortable in my hand when I gripped it tightly before heading out of the house with the door slamming shut behind me. People were beginning to gather on the sidewalk outside of their homes with the distant sounds of a truck blaring through the streets.

Judging by the way it was echoing against the houses, I'd say it was at least another mile and a half out.

Coming up to the burning house, the heat hit me hard. The fire was contained to the top floor, flames licking out of the open—or rather shattered—window while climbing up to the worn roof. Black smoke had collected on the bottom level, making it impossible to see inside to check if anyone was still in there.

A neighbor sprinted outside from the house next to it, a phone held up to her ear while she chattered on to dispatch.

I grabbed her arm to stop her from heading across the street. "Who's in there?"

Her eyes were frantic. "I don't know! They're an older couple. I have nine-one-one on the phone!"

Older couple. That wasn't good. That meant there was a potential for either mobility issues or pre-existing health problems. Or both.

"The car is in the driveway!" She pointed to the small car park next to the house. "I think they're still in there!"

Two men from the house across the street were running toward the house— both of them touting leather jackets and bandanas over their mouths. I shoved the woman toward the street again, gesturing for her to wait on the opposite sidewalk while thanking her.

I brandished my axe to the two men, noticing one of them had a pair of heavy duty diving goggles on his head. "Let me borrow those!"

Either I was presenting with a 'don't question me' attitude, or they were glad to have someone leading this thing, because soon I had a pair of goggles shoved into my hands and two guys ready to take orders.

While snapping the lenses over my head, I yelled at them both to get everyone off this side of the street so that when the trucks finally arrived, they weren't trying to crowd manage and get their lines hooked up to the fire hydrant at the same time.

They nodded at me and then sprinted off in opposite directions, corralling people as soon as they got close enough to them. The goggles were tight on my head, but gave enough suction that I wouldn't be tearing up from the smoke burning my eyes.

Getting up to the house, sweat began to pour down my back and arms. Since the top window had already blown out and was creating a vacuum to suck all of the heat out of the top, breaking down this door wouldn't run the risk of causing any kind of backdraft once I got it off its hinges.

My axe cut through the wood solidly, tearing off chunks with each blow. Thankfully, the entire house was old as dirt and gave way easily to a little bit of force from a sharp weapon.

As I pried the door open, smoke began to billow out around me, choking me even through the shirt tied tightly around my nose and mouth.

I stepped back to let the place air out for a few seconds, clearing out as much as possible before moving back toward the opening again.

"Hello!" I called out, carefully stepping inside.

The bottom floor was lit with smoldering embers. Pieces of furniture and all that was left of the carpet were still on fire but had a yellow-y golden hue to them and not the blue-hot like the top floor.

"Hello! Anyone in here!"

Barely above the crackling of the wood around me, I heard a soft cough.

Following it, I almost stepped on him—a man laying face down on the floor.

Tucking the handle of my axe into my belt loop, I bent and scooped my hands under his armpits. He was light compared to what I'd been expecting, clearly much frailer than his height suggested. He coughed again as I dragged him out, kicking back through the chunks of roof that had fallen onto the floor.

Where I found him wasn't that far from the doorway, thankfully, and soon enough, we were back out onto the street.

My lungs burned as I sucked in fresh clean air.

The man in my arms choked and gagged when I set him down. His skin was blackened from the fire and ash that had been coating him by the time I'd found him.

"M… my," the older man let out a deep, chest-y cough. "My wife…"

Behind me a truck docked, several firefighters jumping off and running over to me.

"Cruz!" One of them yelled. "What the fuck are you doing here?"

I wiped at my goggles, spotting Eddie, one of my old coworkers at the fire station. "Take care of him, I think there's one more inside!"

"Hey, wait!" he yelled.

Before he could catch me and wrangle me back in, I sprinted for the open doorway once more, ignoring my training in waiting for my geared up coworkers to take it from here. There was something in me that was telling me that any more time wasted out here catching everyone up to speed was time wasted in pulling this man's wife out of the wreckage alive.

Call it my intuition or hubris.

I slipped the axe up into my hands again and carefully ducked back into the house. There was no sign of the man's wife anywhere, even as I traveled to the spot I'd found him at.

"Hello!" Calling out got me nothing, not even when I heard the telltale signs of water beginning to hit the side of the house to put it out.

"Xavier!" someone yelled into the house from the doorway.

Ignoring them, I continued further, choking as more smoke made it harder to breathe. If there was anyone following after me, I couldn't tell. The sound of the wood paneling was loud as it burned, near ear piercing and making it impossible to think straight.

XAVIER

There was a doorway that led into a small kitchen, almost completely untouched from the rest of the fire by the awkward angle of the house's layout. My heart picked up when I spotted a woman laying face down on the floor, facing away from me.

"Ma'am!" Setting my axe down onto the floor, I rolled her over to pat her face a few times. She didn't flinch at all, not even so much as moved a damn muscle.

I bent down to see if I could hear her breathing, and the sudden cacophony of a ceiling coming down had me jumping back and pressing myself against the cabinets behind me. Debris and smoke suddenly filled the kitchen, making it hard to see where the hell it had fallen.

Waving my arm in front of my face did nothing aside from making me feel lightheaded.

The woman next to me groaned softly.

Oh thank fuck.

I scooped her up, noting she was a little heavier than her husband but not by much. I threw her half over my shoulder in a fireman's hold while reaching for my axe and climbing to my feet. As I finally got closer to where I'd come from, I realized a large partition of debris blocked us in, the ceiling having fallen right outside of the entryway into the kitchen.

Looking around, my heart sunk when I discovered there was no other door leading outside—effectively trapping us like sitting ducks.

Fuck.

The window above the sink was our only escape.

Could we even fit?

XAVIER

We have to. There's no other way.

I wasn't going to die in this damn kitchen—nor was I going to let this woman die with me. As a search and rescue firefighter, I had too much experience under my belt to let something like a fallen ceiling blocking mc from the point-of-entry to force me into giving up.

Not when I had a damn kid and boyfriend to get back to.

Shifting the woman's weight on my shoulder, I swung my axe back and shattered the frame and glass all in one go. The glass shards exploded outward, leaving nothing but the remnant pieces still stuck to the frame that I scraped at with the back of my axe head.

It was an awkward angle but I managed to hoist the woman up off of me and out through the window. With a momentary wave of guilt, I shoved her out of the window and winced when I heard her hit the ground outside with a groan.

Well, it was better than burning to death in a fire.

I threw my axe out next hard enough that I knew it would miss her completely and then I catapulted myself up over the sink and onto the ledge of the window. She was on her side, facing away from the house, a pained expression on her face.

Carefully slipping down from the sill, my body pitched forward and I just barely caught myself before I face-planted onto the ground along with her. I was crashing from my adrenaline rush—cut short by the lack of oxygen to my damn brain.

The woman groaned again, clearly feeling how the fire was cooking us by being so close to it. Forcing myself up from the ground, I grabbed her arm and began dragging her around the side of the house, stumbling when above me, another window shattered and rained glass down onto us.

Using my body as a shield to protect her was only so useful when I began to grow dizzy once again.

"Cruz! You fucking idiot!" someone yelled.

My vision blacked out right when a pair of hands grabbed onto me.

"Are you suicidal!" the voice chastised.

Belatedly, I realized it was Eddie.

And then I was gone.

CHAPTER TWENTY-SIX

Gage

THE LAST PHONE call I ever expected to receive was a number out in California that I didn't recognize.

While I had half a mind to ignore it, something nagged at me to answer it. Almost like I had some guardian angel whispering over my shoulder that it had something to do with Xavier.

Because who the hell else did I know

from California that would be calling me this late at night?

"Hello?" I answered.

There was a slight pause on the other end. "Uh, hey, Gage... it's Dexter."

That immediately had me sitting up in my bed. "You okay?"

Alarm bells were going off in my head immediately. There was no reason for Dexter to be calling *me* of all people unless there was some dire emergency going on. Not when Xavier could just do it himself.

I kicked off my covers to roll out of bed and head over to my closet, my heart pounding.

"So... dad was kind of in an accident," Dexter said slowly.

Oh god.

Oh, fuck.

My hands shook while reaching for one of my shirts hanging in the closet. "How bad?"

There was some noise on the other end as the line was muffled. I couldn't tell what it was or if Dexter was talking to someone else to get the information, but either way, I was about ready to throw the fuck up.

Finally when he came back to the phone, he said, "He had a lot of smoke inhalation. They have him on a ventilator."

"Smoke?"

What the fuck was Xavier doing around a goddamn fire the same day he came back from vacation?

What, was his station a bunch of fucking slave drivers?

They couldn't give the man one fucking

day to recover?

"Yeah. He wasn't wearing any gear so it was pretty bad. I guess it was his neighbor?"

Leave it to Xavier to play fucking hero.

"I'll be right there. Can you text me which hospital you're at?"

Dexter sputtered on the other end. "You don't have to come all the way out here. I just wanted to call and let you know so you weren't worried that he wasn't answering your calls or texts."

This kid was too sweet for his own good. Despite all of the bad shit that's happening to him and between him and Xavier, he still cared deeply for his loved ones. I could appreciate that wholeheartedly.

"Dexter?"

"Yeah?"

"Just text me the hospital."

He was silent for a moment. "Okay."

"Great," I said, shoving one of my legs through a pant hole. "I'll see you soon."

XAVIER

CHAPTER TWENTY-SEVEN

Gage

IF CALIFORNIA TRAFFIC had one enemy, it was me. And if California fucking traffic had *no* enemies, then I was fucking dead.

The amount of times Xavier had joked with me that a 'California mile' was actually five disguised with a hat and a trench coat would've given me enough money to buy myself a full week's worth of groceries.

All those times I'd called him out for his over exaggerations and yet here I was, a damn fool for not trusting my very un-sarcastic boyfriend from giving me a harsh reality check in the form of being stuck in jam packed traffic after getting off of a red-eye flight that had me gnawing at the skin around my nails for the entire four and a half hours that it took to get over here.

A damn fool. That's what I was.

By the time my rideshare finally pulled into Mercy General, I was about ready to tear my hair out from all of the stress. Travel had never been my favorite, and doing so when a loved one was laid up in the hospital on a ventilator made all of that ten times fucking worse.

I'd loosely been texting Dexter since

he'd called me, thankful for the small updates he'd been giving me so that I wasn't losing my ever loving mind with worry that I was going to arrive to a cadaver already toe-ticketed inside of the morgue downstairs.

Xavier was up on the third floor. There was no actual timeline for him waking up or being taken off of the ventilator but his brain activity was very healthy despite his dangerous dip in oxygen levels.

With my heart in my throat, I took the elevator up while sending Dexter a quick text that I was here. I hated the not knowing everything about all of this. While the good news was good, the bad news is what scared me the most.

Xavier being in any kind of coma freaked me right the hell out. Even if the doctors were hopeful that he would wake up soon.

What if he didn't?

What if I was walking into a situation where I was actually saying goodbye to him?

I was never going to be able to handle something like that. I'd shatter into a million pieces if I didn't go home with Xavier still alive.

To my surprise, when the elevator doors opened up, Dexter was standing there waiting for me. He perked up as soon as he spotted me, lifting himself away from the wall to meet me in the middle of the hallway.

"Hey..." I said, my hands itching to reach out and hug him. Despite us only knowing each other a short while, I still felt a connection to Dexter. My brothers liked him, my boyfriend adored him.

Therefore in my mind, he was already family.

"Your flight go okay?" he asked.

I blew out a breath in response.

See, the thing about getting a last minute flight wasn't that the prices were astronomical or that the seat you got assigned to you was of course at the very back of the plane next to the bathrooms. No, the worst part was that taking a red-eye meant you had half the passengers sleeping peacefully and the other half being absolute and downright weirdos.

My luck, I'd been seated between two.

"I made it," was what I finally settled on.

He nodded in response and then pivoted on his heel to lead me back down the hallway. Nurses and doctors moved all about the floor, coming and going in and out of rooms that we passed by. There wasn't so much of a frantic energy to the place as there was a purposeful one.

Which actually made me feel a little bit better. With no codes being called, that meant that everyone here was stable. For now.

Dexter stopped in front of a room that was kitty corner to the nurses' station, the door already propped open.

He led me inside with a wave, stepping back so I could enter before him.

My heart leaped into my chest when I caught sight of Xavier on the bed. His eyes were closed with a tube shoved down his throat. On either side of him were a bunch of monitors that beeped softly, tracking all sorts of things that I couldn't exactly wrap my head around at this point.

No one else was in the room, thankfully.

"They said he's going good," Dexter said from behind me, his voice soft. "I know it looks bad from here."

Yeah, that was an understatement. But I appreciated the sentiment regardless. Dexter was a pretty aware guy, even for just seventeen. I think he got that from his dad, honestly. That man could read you like a damn first grade level book.

My feet carried me over to his bedside. As long as I ignored the giant tube coming out of his mouth, he looked like he was peacefully sleeping.

"I should've brought flowers or something," I joked, my voice sounding hollow. "This place is so drab."

"I think there are some bouquets down in the gift shop," Dexter supplied.

He really was such a sweet kid.

Nodding, I scooped up Xavier's hand into mine, squeezing it lightly so that I wouldn't disturb the IV-line taped to the top of it. His hand was warmer than I was expecting, relieving the tension that had been building inside of my chest just a little bit more.

Leaving in a flurry earlier had both scared the twins and made them want to come with me. I'd barely gotten them to agree to staying behind and looking after the house while I jetted off to California for the foreseeable future.

I felt guilty leaving them behind, or at all, with them having such limited time to spend with me before they both had to leave for their respective careers again. No matter how many times they'd reassured me while they drove me to the airport, I still felt bad.

This wasn't exactly what either of them signed up for when coming home to visit me right before the holidays.

Leave it to Xavier to play hero and cause us all to be scared to death.

"Dexter," a woman's voice called from the doorway. "We brought you some food from the—who the hell are *you*?"

I dropped Xavier's hand instantly, whipping around to see a blonde haired woman glaring at me as she held a tray of cellophane wrapped food. Behind her, a man with glasses also ducked into the room, stopping short at seeing me just as she had.

Oh fuck.

Why didn't I figure that Dexter hadn't

come alone to the hospital?

The kid was seventeen with no driver's license. Obviously, he'd be here with his mother and... stepdad?

"Uh," was all that came out of my mouth.

"This is Gage," Dexter said, waving a hand at me. "Dad's boyfriend."

Instantly, my face heated up.

Oh, man...

I'd never had that whole 'coming out to your parents' experience since by the time I'd figured out that I was down and dirty for the same sex, mine were long gone and buried in the dirt. The closest I'd ever come was bringing a boy home to my brothers and introducing them both to him as my 'special friend' until they were old enough to start calling me out on my bullshit.

But here, with Dexter presenting me to his mother as her ex's significant other, gave me a good slap of reality to what that all might've been like. The embarrassment that no straight kids would ever feel. The anxiety over potentially being rejected. The fear that hatred would follow.

All of this was a mix of emotions that I hadn't been expecting to feel, let alone confront, once I stepped off that plane and into the horrid desert heat.

"O-Oh." His mother cleared her throat. "Um... how did you know he was here?"

"I called and told him," Dexter said.

"*Why* would you do that?" His step-dad frowned.

To his credit, Dexter simply answered him with a very bored, "Because they've been dating for a year and he deserved to know."

When both adults turned to look at me again, all I could think to do was plaster a, hopefully, pleasant looking smile on my face. "It's nice to meet you. Uh, sorry for the conditions."

Dexter's mother, Kate, sighed. She looked worn, like she'd been up all night talking to the doctors and taking care of Xavier. I didn't want to assume much, given that my... *opinion* of Kate wasn't the greatest.

However, she did bring Dexter down here to see him. So...

Maybe she wasn't a total lost cause.

"Gage..." Kate mumbled, not exactly looking at me. "How long are you planning on staying?"

I shrugged.

Not really the most solid of answers but the truth nonetheless. I was determined to stay here until the man lying on that hospital bed—the love of my life—finally opened his eyes. Leaving any sooner would just cause me to have a massive meltdown while I stressed about him never waking up again.

She sighed again. "All right... Well, I'm Kate. This Dan, my husband. You already know my son?"

"Uh..." Glancing over at Dexter was no fucking help as he only gave me a 'you're on your own' kind of shrug. "Yeah... Xavier and I... we introduced our kids to each other when things got serious. So..."

Not a total lie.

Plus, if Xavier, or Dexter, hadn't told her about the college thing yet, I wasn't about to spill the beans in the middle of a hospital room with a man hooked up to a damn ventilator in the background.

"You have kids?" her husband asked, running his gaze up and down me. "How many?"

"Two? Well, okay. They're not *my* kids. They're my younger twin brothers, but we have a pretty big age gap so I consider them mine since I've been raising them by myself for close to a decade."

Both Kate and her husband looked shocked to hear that, along with a little bit impressed. I suppose maybe to a secular couple, hearing something like that was quite admirable. Taking on the task of raising kids that you didn't birth yourself got me all kinds of praise, even if I never asked or wanted it.

Coming from a religious couple, that kind of shit was downright celebrated.

Or at least from what I've heard. I was not exactly a connoisseur of religious upbringings.

"How old are they?" Kate asked.

"Nineteen. One of them enlisted and the other is working on a horse ranch." I grin. "I'm quite proud."

To my surprise, Kate's expression softened.

She didn't say anything to that, just simply nodded before turning to Dexter to offer him one of the sandwiches on the tray and a small bottle of juice she'd grabbed for him. Her husband walked around her to settle into one of the chairs over by the window, unwrapping his own sandwich in his lap.

Ugh, this was so awkward. I kind of wished Dexter had warned me his parents would be here before I'd shown up. Then again, maybe he knew better than to let me get into my head about it and decided that blindsiding me was the better way to go about it.

Or maybe I was reading way too far into this entire situation. Kind of like I usually did with everything else.

"I'll eat in a bit, mom," Dexter said, setting his sandwich down on the windowsill. "Gage wanted to go grab dad some flowers from the gift shop, so I'm going to go show him where it is."

Kate looked like she was ready to argue but then glanced over at me and deflated almost as quickly. "All right... Just be back here in half an hour. Gage, I want your phone number."

"Oh. Yeah, sure." I pulled out my phone to exchange numbers with her, aware that Dexter was hovering close by.

Once we were all set, I flashed her another smile and then headed back out into the hallway with her son tagging next to me. Halfway to the elevator, I looked back to see Kate leaning out the doorway, watching us both like a hawk.

I kind of felt bad that she was so paranoid. Though, I guess knowing what I knew now with what happened to Dexter, I couldn't exactly blame her.

So, instead of feeling the kind of annoyance I usually would whenever Xavier brought Kate up, I waved to her and lifted up my phone, gesturing to it with a thumbs up.

Her shoulders seemed to sag at that, a small nod following before she ducked back into the room.

Dexter pressed the button for the elevator, watching me closely. "She means well... I think."

I glanced over at him. "Tough crowd?"

He rolled his eyes. "You have no idea. This is her being good."

"If it makes you feel any better, I'm ten times worse with the twins."

"Forgive me if I don't actually believe you," he said right as the elevator doors popped open.

Grinning, I waited for him to get in first before following after and letting my body sag against the metal wall. Damn, those airline seats were no joke these days. When the hell did they get so *small*?

"Thanks for calling me, by the way." I said.

"No need to thank me. I do kind of want you to stick around, so I figured letting you into the family drama was a good start."

"Aw, does that mean Dexter approves of me?"

He shot me a look. "Well, if I want to go to LSU, I should probably make friends with the locals."

I laughed. "It's a good school. I'm not going to knock it. Besides, I definitely wouldn't hate if you and your dad moved closer to me. The traffic out here sucks."

Dexter snorted. "Yeah, try living here."

When the doors opened up again, I had to shuffle to the side to make room for the onslaught of people pushing their way into the small, cramped space. Both of us managed to slip out into the lobby, barely missing us being trapped behind the closing doors and being skated up to whatever floor was next on the chopping block.

The front lobby to Mercy General was nice, if not a little boring. Though, I supposed as far as hospitals went, that wasn't exactly a bad thing.

Dexter waved for me to follow him, leading me down the main entryway to a large gift shop that was located right as you walked into the hospital. Thankfully, it was much quieter trapped behind these glass walls.

I spotted the flowers toward the back of the shop—located in a small corner that had a bodega-like set-up with a few buckets of premade bouquets and then a few that had loose stems you could put together yourself.

I opted for the loose ones, grabbing a pre-cut piece of decorative cellophane to wrap the stems in.

Dexter hovered next to me, nodding in approval or shaking his head with each flower I held up. Together, we put together a nice looking bouquet that was both colorful but not too flashy for a 'get well soon' sentiment.

"Nice," I said, holding it up while Dexter tied a piece of twine around it.

He smiled at the flowers, leaning in to breathe in their scent. "I think he'll like thcm."

"Me too. Would you believe me if I said I never got someone flowers before?"

Dexter snorted. "So dad will be your first? You should tell him when he wakes up. He's a secret sap."

"Secret or covert?"

That had Dexter smiling again.

We headed up to the register, getting in line behind an older woman and her husband who was holding her hand. The sight was sweet, reminding me of all the sappy love stories I couldn't help to daydream about whenever I thought of

Xavier.

Which was often to an embarrassing level.

One would think that after a solid year, I would've gotten over the butterflies by now.

"Were you serious about living with dad?" Dexter asked.

Turning to him, I raised a brow. "Only if he wants to."

He stared at me for a long moment. "Why haven't you already?"

"He didn't want to leave you behind and not see you."

"What about after I'm gone?"

I shrugged. "We'll see. I'm trying not to be pushy."

"But you *want* to be," he guessed.

Holding back a groan took monumental effort. See, knowing Xavier, I knew exactly where Dexter got his smarts from, as well as his keen eye. What I *didn't* like was when it was turned on *me*.

"Did he bring up the marriage thing yet?" Dexter asked. "I told him to."

Balking, I said, "Dexter. Leave the matchmaking up to the adults."

He rolled his eyes at me. "What's four months going to change? I'll still think the same way, you know."

"What, that you want me and your dad to get married?"

"I want him to be *happy*." He sounded annoyed as he spoke. "He needs to stop focusing all his energy on me. What's going to happen when I go to college? I don't want him dropping dead like a fly because he no longer has a purpose anymore."

I loved hearing that Dexter cared about

his dad just as much as Xavier cared about him. Not that I had any doubts that deep down inside, their bond had yet to be totally shattered despite Xavier's constant worrying that he'd fucked up beyond repair.

Seeing Dexter just as protective over his dad was a welcome sight, one that I hoped Xavier got to see one day. It would at least show him that trying to mend this bridge was worth it in the end; that getting sober and taking back his life had gotten him his son back.

And wasn't that a goddamn beautiful thing?

Taking the chance, I reached up to ruffle his hair in the way I always did with my brothers. "Anyone ever tell you that you're a sour patch kid?"

He batted my hand away, though his

expression was more bemused than anything. "What's that even mean?"

"First you're sour," I said, reciting the commercial. "Then you're sweet."

"Funny," he said, fighting hard to not crack a smile.

"I really am, aren't I?"

Once we got up to the counter and paid for the bouquet, we wandered around the shop for a few more minutes before braving the crowds and heading back up to Xavier's floor. By the time we arrived, Dexter's stepfather was passed out in his chair while his mother scrolled on her phone, popping her head up as soon as we entered.

She eyed the flowers in my hand warily but said nothing when I placed them down onto the bedside table to Xavier's left hand side. They looked nice against the rather drab colored room, bringing a little bit of life to the place despite the somber mood.

Dexter dragged a chair over for me to sit in, pulling his own right alongside mine.

"And now we wait," he mumbled to me, settling back into his chair.

I sighed in agreement.

Hopefully, not for long.

CHAPTER TWENTY-EIGHT

Xavier

FAINT VOICES WERE what broke through the darkness surrounding me. They were hard to make out, the words blurring together with one another while the tones were stilted and disfigured.

I concentrated on them, trying to pull myself up from the void that had swallowed me, figuring that following it would lead me back into the light.

"You should go." One of them was a little more distinct—closer, maybe. *"It's the holidays."*

"But what about you?" Younger sounding.

Where even was I?

Nothing around me looked familiar. Or rather, I couldn't *see* anything that looked familiar.

Had that fire blinded me?

Going in with no gear on had been stupid, I'd give myself that much. The thing about blazes catching so quickly and with civilians inside—elders at that—seconds could mean life or death.

Choosing to go in there with no plan aside from listening to the sheer adrenaline pumping through my veins was what saved those two. At least, that's what I'd like to hope. I'd passed out before

I could make sure they were both taken to the ER.

Shit.

Was I *dead*?

"It's okay. I'll be fine. I'll call you guys if anything changes." That voice again. Something else was distorted, hard to piece together while I concentrated on the voices that were drowned out by a subtle beeping sound.

Someone sighed.

"Are you sure?" A woman's voice this time.

Something squeezed my hand. I looked down at it—couldn't see it.

"Yeah, all good. Hope you guys have a good rest of your Christmas."

Christmas?

Oh, fuck.

"You too, Gage."

Gage.

"Bye, dad. See you soon."

Dexter!

I was missing fucking Christmas. I couldn't believe this.

How fucking long had I been out for?

Arriving home with Dexter, there had still been a few days before the holiday. *And* I was making Gage miss it with me.

How the fuck was he even here?

Pieces began to slide together as I traveled further into the darkness, pushing my way through it so I could get back to my kid and boyfriend. Dexter must've called him—probably not wanting him to worry. My kid was always so thoughtful, even if he preferred for people not to see that side of him.

He'd gotten that from his mother. His heart worn on his sleeve, no matter how hard he tried to conceal it from the world.

The beeping was getting louder, more distinct. I followed it. Followed the sounds around me and the hand that squeezed mine in a vice grip. I needed to get back to where I belonged. Back to the people I loved.

CHAPTER TWENTY-NINE

Xavier

WAKING UP TO a ventilator tube shoved down my throat wasn't as bad as it was getting it forcibly removed by two nurses—one pulling and the other on standby with a bucket under my chin, ready to catch whatever vomit or mucus, or both, that I ended up coughing up as soon as the tube was free from my body.

I choked while gripping the side of the

bucket, all but drooling into it as my body fought to pull in oxygen with my own muscles around the heaving coughing fits that wracked my body.

Fuck, was that a bitch and a half.

One of the nurses was slapping me on the back a few times, breaking up whatever had settled in my lungs as I choked it up while the other one was cheerfully giving Gage the rundown on aftercare.

The sad part about all of this wasn't that I could've damaged my lungs permanently by being an idiot and running into a burning building. No, it was that I didn't regret a damn thing. Saving those people had been worth it to me, despite it costing me a few days being unconscious and right now, a bit of my dignity.

XAVIER

Spitting out the last of it, I grabbed the towels that were handed over to me and lifted my hand out to Gage who was hovering nearby, an anxious look etched onto his face.

He took my hand quickly, squeezing it tight just like he had to wake me up. While I felt bad that he'd flown all the way over here in order to be by my side during all of this, I was damn happy that he'd come all this way just for *me*.

Him missing his Christmas with the twins was unfair, yet at the same time I was selfishly glad I had my partner with me, or else I'd probably be losing my damn mind right about now.

"We'll go inform the doctors that you're awake," one of the nurses said, flashing a smile at me. "They'll want to run your levels again, but so far, you're looking really good."

Well, that was a relief at least.

"Thank you," Gage told them on my behalf.

When they left, he blew out a long breath and then collapsed down onto the edge of the bed. I tugged him over toward me using our laced hands, letting him fall into my shoulder and sag against me completely until he was closer to jello than human man.

I brushed my lips over his temple while I breathed him in. I could actually cry right now, I was so damn happy.

"Merry Christmas," he said, laughing softly.

"I'm sorry," I whispered back.

My throat was still incredibly raw from the tube, making it hard to say anything above a whisper. Gage could hear me all the same though, turning slightly to press his nose against the underside of my jaw.

He breathed out slowly again, his fingers flexing around mine.

I knew this side of him well. His anxiety was finally crashing and now all that was left was relief and exhaustion. If I could offer him more room on this bed to pass out on, I would. Unfortunately, we were both fully grown large men and these beds were only meant to fit medium sized people at best.

"The boys wanted me to wish you a Merry Christmas on their behalf," he mumbled.

I pressed another kiss against his head. Too bad they hadn't come with him. I understood why, of course, especially with how long I was out for.

Still, that didn't make it any less

bittersweet.

"Dexter and his mom and stepdad were here this morning," Gage went on. "They didn't want to leave in case you woke up, but I told them they should go celebrate their day together. It's Dexter's last Christmas with them, most likely, so I didn't want them missing that. Sorry for sending them away, I really thought you'd be under still."

I shook my head. "S'okay."

He'd made the right call. Don't get me wrong, I would've loved to wake up with him and Dexter both at my side, however making Dexter sit in a hospital room all day when he should be enjoying the holiday just as Gage had said was a much better option in my opinion.

Was I upset I was also missing the holiday with him?

Absolutely. Gage was, too, so at least we were together on that front.

"The boys..." I mumbled.

"Oh, don't worry. They already ripped through all their gifts and sent me photos and videos." He chuckled. "I swear, I gave them the okay and not even a minute later, I was receiving updates on what they got."

That was good to hear. At least the boys would be at Gage's until New Years Day. Gage would get a little holiday time with them before they were back out in the world.

"You know..." When he lifted himself up, he shifted around until he was facing me, his side resting against the back of the bed. He kept our fingers entangled in a tight grip. "Since we're both missing Christmas, we should do something for

New Years."

I raised a brow and mouthed, "Together?"

He nodded. "Yeah, why not? Unless you have some other hot date I don't know about."

Funny, I wanted to say, settling for a look instead. He was lucky I couldn't talk and was too stiff to tug him over to kiss those jealous thoughts right out of him.

Instead, I settled on lifting his hand up to my lips and pressing a kiss against it. His smile was radiant, eyes soft despite the dark circles under them.

When I was finally discharged from this place, we were going to go back to my place and I was going to force this man into my bed to actually sleep, regardless of the inevitable begging to take care of me.

XAVIER

"Is that a yes? The station pushed back the date for the Christmas party. I guess they were too worried about what was going on with you to be in the mood to throw a holiday party. So now it's going to be a joint Christmas/New Years extravaganza."

That was sweet. I knew how much Gage was looking forward to the party. Now, instead of him having to go stag, I'd get to accompany him. Turning him down the first time had killed me, even more so when that hopeful look in his eyes had faded and was replaced by abject sadness.

I nodded firmly, showing him my decision to the question.

When he grinned, I couldn't help mirroring it with my own. "Okay, awesome. I'll let the gang know. They're so excited to meet you. I may have been bragging about how handsome you are, so if you get stared at a lot, that's totally my bad."

I held back a snort, kissing his hand again.

Meeting Gage's crew would certainly be interesting.

He'd talked about them enough over the past year and a half, that at this point, I felt like I practically already knew them, too. I was glad to hear that they were eager to meet me—it made things a lot easier when bringing a newbie into such a tight-knit work environment.

Especially, if one day I did end up moving out there and needed to find a job. I wouldn't mind setting my roots down at Station Twenty-One for as long as they'd have me.

XAVIER

I wouldn't mind setting my roots down in Baton Rouge for as long as *Gage* would have me.

He sunk back into my side, resting his head against my shoulder, his eyes slowly sliding shut. There was a content smile on his lips that I wished I could take a picture of to immortalize forever.

This man had been through hell and back with me so many times since we'd met, all without a single damn complaint. And I'm sure he'd do it a hundred more times if I ever asked.

Glancing down at our laced fingers, I brushed my thumb down along the bridge of his hand, an idea occurring to me.

Before we took off for Baton Rouge, I needed to swing by *Keeton's.*

CHAPTER THIRTY

Gage

"ARE YOU SERIOUS?"

I swung my bag up onto the bed, and the damn thing's zipper popped open once again. Rolling my eyes, I tossed my phone down next to it in order to grab both sides to force them back together. Wrestling a zipper closed while my bag was overstuffed was the worst fucking task to do by myself.

Xavier had mysteriously left early this morning with hardly any explanation while I'd still been half asleep. By the time I'd realized it, it'd been well past an hour.

I swore that man had no off switch. Two days out of the hospital and he was already trying to run marathons again.

"You don't have to go," I said down to my phone. "I only wanted to pass along the offer since Grey and Ash were asking me to."

Dexter let out a soft noise on the other end of the line, causing me to smile.

How funny was it that he went from having no friends to two that were up my ass about inviting him to the Christmas/New Years extravaganza?

The second they'd heard about me bringing Xavier home with me, they'd shot me back with a *'well, what about Dexter?'*

that I thought was so fucking adorable I could barely contain myself.

Since they were little kids, they'd always talked about having a younger sibling, which, unfortunately, never came to fruition after the death of our parents. Now, with Dexter in the picture, it seemed like they were determined to adopt him under their wings.

"You're actually serious?"

I rolled my eyes again. "I can have them Facetime you and have them ask you themselves."

He grunted at me, no doubt with a finger shoved into his mouth and halfway through chewing apart a cuticle. He'd done that a lot at the hospital, anytime he thought no one was paying attention to him. By Christmas, the poor skin around his nails was ripped to shreds.

Did I blame him at all?

Nope, not one bit. Hell, I'd been bouncing off the walls the entire three days Xavier had been passed out. By that fourth day, just before he finally woke up, even *I* was ready to start taking up a bad habit.

"Come on," I goaded. "You know you want to come."

He sighed softly. "Yeah..."

I grinned, finally getting my zipper closed and grabbed my phone. "Awesome. Pack a bag for a few days. I can have your dad talk your mom into letting you come since you got to spend Christmas with them."

Dexter let out a soft snort. "Was that why you kicked us out on Christmas? So you could have leverage?"

"No."

XAVIER

Maybe.

It wasn't intentional.

At the time, at least.

I'd actually wanted them all to spend the day with each other like families were supposed to. Not be stuck in a hospital room cramped in those god awful chairs while we all stared at Xavier's machines and twiddled our thumbs waiting in silence.

Even now, I kind of felt bad taking Dexter away from his mother for New Years; however, at the same time, Xavier deserved a holiday with him, too. During my time in the hospital and getting to know Kate a little bit better, she'd shown me that she wasn't *as bad* as I'd made her out to be in my head.

There were still some sensible bones left in her body, even if her husband did try to scripture me to death at one point.

Thankfully, I'd perfectly the art of *tuning things out,* thanks to my brothers.

"Uh huh," Dexter drawled. "All right, I'll pack a bag and have it by the door. You and dad got all your stuff ready now?"

"For the most part. Your dad ran off a few hours ago to do god knows what. He's barely answered my texts all day, aside from telling me he was heading downtown somewhere."

Tossing my phone back onto the bed, I looped the handle of my bag over my shoulder to carefully set it down by the door. With my luck, any kind of jostling would pop that damn zipper right back open and then I'd be starting all over again.

"Downtown?" There was a pause. And

then, "Oh."

My gaze traveled back to my phone to squint at it.

What did *that* tone mean?

"What?"

"Nothing," he said quickly, flagging my suspicions even further.

Honestly, did I want to know?

No doubt it'd have something to do with the twins and planning some elaborate prank that was either going to embarrass me or piss me off. Such is the way with little brothers and their funny ways with showing that they were going to miss their elder sibling.

Ugh, whatever.

"I'll let your dad know you said yes to coming."

"Thanks," he said. "Text me when you're on your way."

EVIE RILEY

CHAPTER THIRTY-ONE

Gage

THE FLIGHT FROM California to Baton Rouge, while long, hadn't been terrible.

Xavier and I had opted for the 'comfort' seats toward the front of the aircraft instead of suffering with the rest of economy being crammed in the back with little to no leg room and some kid kicking at the back of our seats for the entire damn flight.

Dexter had lucked out and had gotten to have his row, which had been right across from ours, all to himself and used it to his full advantage.

Luckily, I'd gotten a few hours of shuteye while we'd been in the air, only having been shaken awake when the meal service rolled through and Xavier encouraging me to eat something before we landed.

Since getting back from his little impromptu shopping trip, he'd been acting... off. I couldn't quite put my finger on it, but there was something there that I was picking up on that was definitely fishy.

It was bothering the fuck out of me, but anytime I pointed it out, he'd waved me off and distracted me with some kind of kiss or brush of his hand over my body that had those weird feelings melting away instantly.

I supposed it made more sense for him to be acting this way with the looming issue of him meeting my coworkers in less than a few hours.

No matter how many stories I told about them or tried to prepare him for the absolutely ridiculousness that he was about to be walking into, the full picture wouldn't reveal itself until *after* he got there and saw for himself exactly what I had to deal with day in and day out.

Look, I could only do so much.

At least we had a few hours to ourselves to chill at my place before that.

De-boarding and heading back through security was a breeze. I'd called my brothers ahead of time to meet us at the terminal since I'd left my car with them and like *fuck* I was going to pay for a rideshare that would charge me an arm, a leg, and my left kidney just to be picked up from the airport.

Cramming us all into my little sedan wasn't going to be fun, but it beat paying an entire goddamn paycheck to get home.

"You sleep okay?" Xavier ran a hand through the back of my hair as we stepped onto the escalator heading down to the front lobby.

"Yeah. Wasn't too bad. Did you sleep at all?"

"Wasn't tired."

I narrowed my eyes at him. Wasn't tired, my ass, tell that to the bags under his eyes.

What was going on with him today?

I'd blame it on the jet lag but this had been going on since this morning. There was no way I was reading into things when the red flags were waving themselves right in front of my face.

Just as I was about to point out the hypocrisy in his statement, I caught Dexter on the step above us squinting at something.

"Oh," Dexter said, folding his arms over his chest. "So, it's definitely a Torres thing, then."

My brow popped up at that. "What is?"

By the time I turned around to find whatever he was staring at over my shoulder, there were already people huffing out laughs ahead of us. I scanned the lobby, spotting two familiar teenagers who were holding a comically large sign over their heads.

Their expressions were stone cold while they stared down anyone passing by them and snagging a photo.

The sign read: 'Welcome Home From Prison. Remember to stay away from the goats!' in big bold-as-fuck letters.

Oh my god.

I'm going to kill them.

"Quite the welcome," Xavier noted, an amused look on his face.

I stomped down the last two steps as the escalator folded together and stormed over to them, aware of more people walking by and laughing. When they caught sight of me, they quickly turned themselves toward me, the giant sign bending slightly at the top before straightening out once more.

"You two are so ridiculous," I said, quickly grabbing at one of the sides to rip it from them.

Asher cracked first. "Welcome home,

big bro. Did you miss us?"

"Hey, Xavier. Dexter," Greyson greeted my travel companions.

"Ugh." I worked quickly to roll the sign into a tight cylinder, and then used it to smack both of them. "I'm returning all of your Christmas gifts."

They both gasped in unison.

"You can't do that," Asher argued.

"Yeah, we're already using them all," Greyson said.

"Get," I said, pointing to the sliding doors with the sign.

Sharing a look with each other that wasn't at *all* remorseful, they quickly jogged for the doors, waving Dexter to follow along with them. Shaking my head, I grabbed Xavier's hand when he brushed it against mine and laced our fingers together.

"They're going to be the death of me, I swear."

He chuckled and pressed a kiss against my forehead. "They'll be keeping you on your toes until you're ninety."

I smacked him next with the sign. "Don't curse me like that."

"Too late."

Despite the weird attitude shift in him today, I was so damn happy he was going to be coming with me to the holiday party. The second Ellie had heard about me rushing to California after his accident, she'd immediately rallied everyone into sending me their well wishes, along with postponing the party indefinitely.

Honestly, getting those texts and calls from my work family had me choked up for hours afterward. Knowing that they cared for me was an everyday thing, but seeing it all in textual proof had been even better.

It reminded me that no matter what I was going through, I could always count on them.

One day, I really hoped that if Xavier moved out here to be with me, he'd find his own place at the station just like I had. We were our own brand of wild, ridiculous, and a little fucked up. Perfect for a newcomer like Xavier to join our ranks.

"Ready for the swamp?" I joked as soon as we reached the doors.

"As long as you're suffering with me," Xavier said, tugging me out into the afternoon sun of Baton Rouge.

CHAPTER THIRTY-TWO

Xavier

BREATHING OUT SLOWLY for the fifth time since putting on my dress pants and pressed button up, I checked my pocket one last time to keep myself from fidgeting. The party was in full swing, Gage's coworkers meandering around the fire station while classic holiday music blasted from a small boom box over by the refreshments table.

The place was tastefully decorated with both Christmas and New Years in mind. Normally, the mismatching green and red against the gold would come across as tacky, but they'd somehow pulled it off to create a seamless look.

There were two couples dancing in the middle of the station to the music, looking like they were having the time of their lives as they laughed and spun around to pass their partners back and forth. My gaze tracked Dexter, who was deeply engrossed in a game of cards with Gage's captain, one of the paramedics—a feminine-looking young man that kept popping M&Ms in his mouth every few moments and whose name was apparently Newt, and the twins.

I'd been a little nervous taking Dexter to a gathering like this. Mainly, because

I'd been afraid of him getting overwhelmed and feeling out of place amongst a bunch of people he'd never met before. The twins had taken him on a tour around the entire station, introducing him to the crew one by one while keeping him squished between the both of them.

I was so damn proud of him for taking Gage up on his offer in spending New Years with us. After what happened at the botanical gardens, I was sure I'd have a shut-in on my hands.

But of course, like always, Dexter surprised the fuck out of me.

"You doing okay over here?"

I looked over to the woman approaching me who had a kind smile on her face; Ellie, if I remembered correctly. She nodded at the untouched drink in my hand. "Don't tell me it's flat. I swear, I had them throw in two entire bottles of soda."

Cracking a smile, I said, "No, it's great. This whole thing is."

"Really? I'm glad. I was worried it was going to be a total disaster."

"Not at all. Couldn't even tell you guys pushed it back. Thanks for doing that, by the way. Gage was really excited that he didn't miss anything."

She laughed. "I don't know about that. I think he was more excited that he got to bring you along."

I actually didn't know what to say to that. Obviously, Gage had told me his feelings about wanting me to come and the disappointment that followed after I'd turned him down. But hearing it from someone else that he'd wanted to introduce me to everyone here, had me feeling almost honored in a way.

XAVIER

We were obviously serious—at least, I hoped we fucking were or else I was going to be embarrassing the fuck out of myself here in a little bit—and still, having someone else realize it, too, was almost like a confirmation that our relationship was real to not just us, but everyone else as well.

I'd spent a lot of my life denying my true self. Twenty years ago, I never would've imagined that I'd be here, standing in a fire station and talking to a woman—a *stranger*—about the man I was in a relationship with. That I was in love with. All the while I had a hole burning in my pocket.

It was funny how things could change so much in such a short amount of time.

For the better.

"Everything okay over here?"

Both of us looked back to see Gage smiling at us with a slightly wary expression on his face. His preternatural instincts were off the chart sometimes. Especially, when it came to me. He'd been trying to suss me out all day and, thankfully, hadn't done anything that had gotten me to crack.

I'd come close, but hadn't folded completely.

Yet.

"All good," I said, looping an arm around his waist as soon as he got close enough. "Surprised you guys haven't gotten any calls tonight."

Both of them groaned at me.

"Don't jinx us!" Gage huffed.

"Too late. He already said the words." Ellie frowned.

Oops.

XAVIER

Someone clinking a glass with a metal utensil brought all of our attention to the opposite side of the station where two men, Jase and Quinn, from what I remembered of Gage introducing them to me, were grinning with a bunch of streamers and large plastic glasses in the shape of the New Year's date in their hands.

"Mayor just called and said that the fireworks are a go in five."

Captain Clarke shoved himself up from the card table to clap his hands together loudly, gathering everyone's attention quickly. "All right, everyone. Out front on the driveway will be the best spot. Let's get a move on."

My heart began to pound in my chest. I barely felt Gage squeeze me before he parted from me to grab us both a couple of streamers and two plastic glasses to put on. We waited until the boys were heading for the door with their own sets, following closely behind them as we all exited the firehouse and stood out on the triple-wide driveway.

A bunch of people were already waiting on the sidewalk facing the eastern night sky. Some of them were already setting off sparklers and waving them around in the air, while others were lounging in folding chairs.

"Are the fireworks big this time of year?" Dexter asked while taking a pair of glasses from Asher.

"Oh, the mayor pays for a crazy display," Gage said, sliding his own glasses over his face. "It's going to blow your mind."

Snorting, I settled mine on top of my

head, needing the unobstructed view of my surroundings while I got my bearings in gear.

Jesus, I was so fucking nervous it was a wonder I wasn't sweating through this damn button up. Or that Gage hadn't noticed and called me out on how antsy I was. He'd been giving me looks all night but had kept his mouth shut, thankfully.

I really wasn't sure what I would've done if he actually called me out and demanded for me to spill the beans on what the fuck was wrong with me. There was no way I would've kept this secret long enough to lie to him.

I'd barely kept it together on the damn plane.

Dexter waved one of the streamers in the air in front of him, glancing over at me with a knowing look. He'd obviously guessed by now and was doing his best to keep the heat off of me with the twins—something I was eternally grateful for.

"One minute!" someone called out.

Oh, fuck.

"Hey," Gage's arm looped around mine. "You okay? You're sweating."

"Swamp weather, babe," I muttered at him, hoping he'd buy the excuse.

He seemed about to argue with me, but was quickly distracted by someone shouting out a countdown, thankfully. He squeezed my arm in his and lifted his streamer into the air and waved it a few times.

Okay, I could do this.

The worst he'd say was 'no'.

Actually, the worst he could say was *hell no.*

Fuck, now I was getting in my head.

XAVIER

This was such an impulsive decision. Three days ago at the hospital it'd felt right. *This morning* had, too.

Now, I was fucking panicking.

"Five! Four!" People began to chant the countdown.

I'd jumped out of planes, for god's sake. I'd been through active combat.

I'd gotten sober.

How the hell could proposing to my boyfriend terrify me more than any of those things combined?

"Three! Two! One! Happy New Year!"

People began to cheer around me. The first flash from a firework lighting up the night's sky shimmered as it broke over the line of buildings in front of us, raining down over the inky blackness with beautiful flakes of white and gold embers.

One by one, fireworks were shot off

from somewhere deeper in the city. From golds, blues, purples, and pinks, they were all mesmerizing to watch explode, illuminating the sky for a brief moment before fading like they were never there to begin with.

I couldn't help but glance over at Gage, enraptured by the way his jaw was slack with awe as he stared at the display. His eyes lit up each time a new one was shot off, the reflection of it mirroring back at me.

"Wow," he breathed out with a soft smile turning up the corners of his lips.

He always found the joy in the little things. I loved that quality about him.

Hell, I loved *everything* about him.

I'd never get enough, no matter how much time passed and how long we spent with each other.

XAVIER

I'd never get tired of any of it.

Before long, fireworks were being shot off in rapid succession, clouding the sky with white smoke as they exploded in unison with each other. People on the sidewalks cheered while the station blew their truck horns and waved their streamers, in anticipation for the final firework.

Unlooping my arm from Gage's caught his attention, causing him to be ripped away from the festivities in order to look over at me.

"Xavier?"

I didn't answer him, and quickly shoved my hand into my pocket to grab at the small box nestled in there. He didn't fight me when I took half a step back from him, his face pinching into one of confusion.

I dropped down to my knee.

The strangled noise spilling out of Gage's mouth was barely audible over the plume of the final firework shooting off into the sky.

I popped the box open, the silver band, hopefully, visible in the dark.

The firework crested high in the sky, the colors of it catching in Gage's eyes when they widened down at me, along with a light shimmering over the ring that he was now staring at incredulously.

"Marry me," I said, just as the explosion from the firework punched through the air and drowned out everything else around us.

The embers rained down in the sky like a gigantic weeping willow, glistening the same way that stars did in the distant galaxy and keeping both of us illuminated just long enough.

"Holy shit," he choked out, pulling in a sharp breath. His hand shot out toward me, splaying his fingers at me. I saw him, rather than heard him, mouth the word 'yes' while the crowd around us cheered loudly at the finale.

His hand was shaking as I took it in mine, popping the band out of the case and carefully sliding it on his finger—a damn perfect fit.

I had to catch him as he fell into me, collapsing with a soft sob. He wrapped his arms tightly around me, burying his face in my shoulder.

With a laugh, I lifted us both back onto our feet, planting my weight back to keep him from toppling us both over.

The lights overhead on the fire station flickered on, announcing the end of the night's festivities and the official beginning of the New Year.

Gage pulled away from me in order to gaze down at the band encircling his finger. He lifted it up to the light to get a better look at it, sniffling. "It's so pretty."

I lifted his hand by the wrist and brought it to my cheek, turning my face to press my lips into his palm. "It has our initials engraved on the inside."

He melted into more tears. "You fucking sap."

That had me laughing and pulling him into a tight hug. Honestly, pot and kettle on that one, but tonight, I'd let him have it.

"Oh, did you do it?" Dexter asked, craning his neck to get a peek at Gage's hand.

Lifting it up into the light again,

nodding with a Cheshire grin on my lips, I showed off the shiny new band, earning a broad smile from my kid, along with two sets of bewildered looks from the twins.

Gage's voice cracked when he turned to look at Dexter. "You knew about this?"

Dexter rubbed the back of his neck. "It was... kind of obvious."

Gage shoved his face against my chest once more, heaving another watery exhale. He was so goddamn cute it was hard not to sweep him up into my arms and carry him back into the damn firehouse where I could find us an empty room.

"Wait, what's happening?" Greyson's gaze darted between Dexter and I.

"My dad proposed." Dexter held out a hand to him, curling his fingers twice. "That means you owe me."

What...

"Shit," Asher muttered, taking out his phone. "You do CashApp?"

The alarm inside of the fire station had us all jumping apart. Flashing lights, along with the piercing sound shattering the quiet of the street, had everyone around us bouncing into action. Two of Gage's coworkers grabbed at the garage door and lifted it open, the rest jogging inside to grab their gear.

"All right, you know the drill!" Captain Clarke called out, following them in. "Let's get a move on, night crew!"

Gage quickly wiped his face, his expression steeling instantly.

Pride bloomed in my chest. "Go get 'em, tiger."

His face faltered for a split second, a small smile tugging at his lips before he schooled it back down. He gave us all a tight nod before spinning on his heel and jogging back into the station.

Asher, Greyson, Dexter, and I kept toward the back with the rest of the plus ones that attended the party. It took the station no time at all to gear up and roll out, the skeleton crew being the only thing left behind after it was all said and done.

Once the door to the garage was pulled closed again, everyone let out a small breath.

While it was no surprise that the station was getting calls from people setting their shit on fire with homemade fireworks displays, I was a little disappointed to have Gage ripped away from me so soon after proposing to him.

A pair of arms wrapped around me

from the side, causing me to look down to see Dexter hugging me.

"Congratulations."

Smiling, I brushed a hand over his head. "Thank you. You think he liked it?" I teased.

"I think you're probably in for another bit of waterworks when he comes home."

Oh, I have no doubt about that.

He pulled away from me with a small smile that turned rather devious when he turned back to the twins. "CashApp you said, right?"

"Shit, he totally remembered," Greyson said, nudging his brother.

Asher nodded. "I was really hoping the fire truck stuff would distract him."

"Nice try," Dexter drawled.

I shook my head at them. "All right, you three brats, get in the car. You can sort out your betting pool when we get home."

CHAPTER THIRTY-THREE

Gage

I ROLLED MY thumb along the underside of my ring for the thousandth time, admiring the smooth metal that felt like silk against my calloused hand.

No matter how many times I touched it, it still didn't feel real.

He'd fucking proposed.

That's why he was acting so goddamn weird. He'd been carrying this ring around in his pocket for who knows how long and I bet it'd been burning a hole in whatever he'd stashed it in until tonight.

No wonder he'd been keeping me at arm's length.

I had to slap my hand over my mouth to keep myself from dancing and screaming as I carefully unlocked my front door and slipped inside. There was a single light on in the foyer to greet me as I came in; an adorable gesture that I had no doubt was from Xavier.

Kicking off my shoes and dropping my gear bag just inside the door, I headed deeper into the house and flicked off the light behind me. The living room was dark, as was the hallway.

Passing by the twin's room and the guest room that was serving as Dexter's room, I saw no light coming from under the crack of either door. Probably a good thing since it was pretty late.

The fire hadn't been horrible to get under control, but had taken forever to get the entire thing put out. By the time we were finished, all of us were exhausted and ready to call it a night.

As I got to my room, I happily noted that the light from under the door spilled out into the hallway. Seeing it made me smile. Xavier waiting up for me wasn't expected, but was appreciated, nonetheless.

While I wouldn't blame him for falling asleep from the jet lag, I also wanted to celebrate with him.

Getting engaged was a big fucking deal!

Popping the door open, I slipped inside as quietly as possible and then closed it behind me without a sound.

Xavier was sitting up in my bed with the covers laid out over his lap and his phone in his hand while he watched something. His head snapped up immediately the moment I stepped into the room, his phone getting tossed to the side in favor of focusing his attention on me.

"How did it go?" he asked, slipping out of bed to come over to me.

I folded myself into his arms, sighing when he pulled me into a tight hug. "Fine. No casualties."

"That's good to hear."

He ran his fingers through my hair, still a little damp from the fast shower I'd taken at the station to get the smell of smoke and sweat off me. Being stuffed inside of my helmet and gear for the past three hours after being brutally assaulted by the scorching heat of a house fire did not produce a smell that would be pleasant for our celebration.

"I can't believe you proposed to me." I still couldn't get any of it out of my head. The way he'd looked kneeling in front of me, how he held out the box to me with the ring inside just as the sky lit up bright with fireworks, or how earnest he'd looked as he'd asked me to marry him.

Ugh!

I was never going to get over it all. Of course, I didn't want to, either.

"Come here," he said, walking us backward to the bed.

I let him lead us, pulling him into a kiss as he turned me around to lay me down on top of my bed. He only broke it briefly to divest me of my clothes, tossing the material away from us and laying me bare before him.

A soft grumble rumbled up inside of his chest as his gaze roamed over me, and he looked pleased at what he saw.

I beckoned him forward with a single finger, loving how easily it was to call him to me. I wrapped my arms around his neck, dragging him down into another kiss.

His tongue rolled along mine, his hips bucking until I spread my legs and wrapped them around his waist.

Fuck, I wanted him so badly.

Xavier was my damn addiction and I didn't even care if that was wrong of me to think.

He trailed his lips down my jawline, leaving wet kisses until he found the sensitive spot on my neck that always made me squirm whenever he sucked on it. He sank his teeth into my skin, sucking and licking as he did so, hard enough that I ground myself up against his hips and begged for a damn release.

At some point, he was going to have to stuff a sock in my mouth because there was no way I was going to be able to remain quiet.

Seeming to read my mind, Xavier's hand curled around my mouth, keeping it locked tight while he sat up. "You going to behave for me?"

I shook my head. I knew my limits too well to pretend like I was any good at obeying them.

He chuckled and took his hand off my mouth in order to tug off his t-shirt. Next, he shoved his sweats down his hips, his cock popping out and bobbing at me.

Automatically, I grabbed onto the back of my knees and brought them up to my chest, exposing myself to him.

His eyes locked onto my hole immediately, his lips parting with lust. "Oh, Gage..."

"Hurry up and fuck your new fiancé. He's tired of waiting."

Xavier let out a soft groan. "Oh, I love the sound of that."

I watched him quickly slip off the bed to retrieve my lube out of the nightstand and then toss it next to me. He kicked off his pants before crawling back onto the mattress, one of his hands clamping down on the back of my thigh to hold me steady.

He drizzled a generous amount of lube over the head of his cock, stroking it downward once before tossing the bottle to the side. His head fell back as he exhaled deeply.

"Put it in me," I begged.

"Fuck," he gritted through his teeth.

Letting go of his cock, he ran two fingers around my puckered holc, tcasing me with each swipe over it. I was desperate for more, *needing* more from him or else I was going to actually explode.

"*Please.* Don't torture me like this."

"You are the prettiest thing I've ever laid my eyes on."

Two fingers slid into me, pumping in and out so deep that his knuckles were breaching my hole with each thrust.

My lashes fluttered shut at the sensations.

Oh, that was good.

But not good enough.

I wanted more from him, I wanted him to bury himself so deep inside of me that I wasn't sure where he ended and I began.

I tightened my hold on my legs, readjusting just enough to keep me from accidentally letting go. Finally, after what felt like forever, Xavier's fingers withdrew from my hole, quickly replaced by the blunt tip of his cockhead.

He leaned over me, a hand coming down over my mouth while his other was still locked onto the back of my thigh. I groaned loudly, thankfully muffled, as he slid into me slowly.

Fuck he was so, so perfect. He stretched me in a way that I'd never had before, his shallow thrusts becoming deeper with each one, until finally, his hips were flush with my ass. His cock twitched inside of me in response to my walls bearing down on him.

My selfish body wanted to keep him inside of me forever. Letting him go was the last option I wanted. He rocked into me, grinding his hips into my ass a few times until I was panting against his hand.

"Ready, fiancé?" he teased.

If he kept calling me that, I wasn't going to last at all.

Nodding at him, I tightened my grip on my legs.

He started off slow, rolling his hips back all the way and then sliding himself home again. His cock glided in and out of me easily, each pass over my prostate had my toes curling and my body twitching.

I loved his cock. I loved him fucking me with it.

I mumbled incoherently against his

hand, getting lost in the pleasure of our bodies coming together after what felt like two long decades of being apart.

We were getting married.

We were *actually* getting married and now we'd never have to be apart ever again. He was going to move here and live with me. Long distance was a thing of the goddamn past now.

My swirling thoughts made me feel giddy.

I let go of my legs to wrap around his waist, pulling him closer to me. His hand was soon replaced with his mouth when he leaned over me, curling his arms under my body to hold me close to his own.

This was what I loved—this closeness—and what I missed when he was gone. I could live in this damn bed forever with this man if given the chance to.

His thrusts became a bit more frantic while his hips slapped against me. I held onto him for dear life, my balls tightening with the need to come.

He reached a hand between us to wrap around my cock and stroke in time with his thrusts. I choked out a moan, bucking my hips up into his hand as cum leaked out of me, coating both of us in the process.

He ripped his mouth off of mine and slammed into me, his body stiffening, warmth filling me as he unloaded into me.

My arms wrapped around him again when he collapsed on top of me. He panted against my neck, sending a shiver skating down my spine.

"So good..." I mumbled.

Xavier kissed my sweat-slicked skin, flashing me a grin. "Happy New Year."

I laughed and held up my hand up in the light to admire my ring again, my heart filling with so much love that I felt my eyes beginning to water once more.

God, I loved this man.

And what an amazing year this one was going to be.

EPILOGUE

Gage

I STOOD IN front of the mirror, trying to adjust my tie for the tenth time. My fingers trembled slightly, making the task more difficult than it should have been. The room was filled with the hum of nervous energy, and I could hear Greyson and Asher chatting animatedly behind me.

The evening was surprisingly chilly,

with a crisp, cool breeze that seemed to seep through the windows and had chased away the usual humidity. The sky outside was a deep, twilight blue, and I could feel the excitement of the coming evening pressing down on me. I'd looked forward to this day for three damn years and I couldn't believe it was finally here.

"I hate these things," I growled.

"Gage, you've got to calm down. You're going to strangle yourself with that tie," Greyson said, his voice filled with amusement as he stepped up beside me. His easygoing nature was a stark contrast to my current state and helped me breathe a little better. Right now, I needed all the help I could get to calm my jangling nerves.

"Here, let me help," Asher chimed in, already reaching out to take over, flitting his fingers at Greyson in a gesture that told his twin to move out of the way. He deftly undid my sloppy knot and started over, his fingers moving with surprising skill.

"Hey, I had it," Greyson whined, punching his brother in the shoulder even as he stepped back to let Asher take over.

How was it my brothers managed to have a knack for being both annoying and endearing at the same time?

Both grown men in their own right now, both with relationships, careers, and homes of their own, Asher settled in Texas and Greyson in Georgia, they still remained the same mischievous twins they'd always been to me. Don't get me wrong, their happiness made my heart soar, but seeing that little bit of the old rivalry tugged at my heartstrings, too.

They were finally grown. I'd done it. Now it was my turn for a happy future and they were both here to support me. Nothing could've made me happier.

"Thanks, Ash," I muttered, sniffling back the tears that threatened behind my eyes and trying to muster a smile. My heart was pounding in my chest, and I could feel the nerves settling in my stomach like a lead weight. "I just... I want everything to be perfect."

"It will be," Greyson said firmly, clapping a hand on my shoulder. "Xavier loves you, Gage. Nothing else matters."

I nodded, trying to take comfort in his words.

Xavier.

Just thinking about him brought a rush of emotions. Love, excitement, and a hint of fear all swirled together, making it hard to breathe. We had been through so much together, and tonight was the culmination of it all.

Our wedding.

The thought of seeing him as I walked down the aisle, of finally pledging our lives to each other, was almost overwhelming.

"You look good, Gage," Asher said, stepping back to admire his handiwork. The tie was now perfectly knotted, sitting neatly against the collar of my crisp, white dress shirt. "Xavier's going to be blown away."

"Yeah, well, let's hope I don't pass out before he gets the chance," I joked weakly, earning a laugh from both of them. Their presence was grounding, a reminder that I was never alone in this.

There was a knock at the door, and

Ellie poked her head in, her eyes bright with unshed tears. "Gage, it's almost time," she said softly. "Are you ready?"

I sucked in a deep breath, letting it out slowly as I glanced at myself once more in the mirror. The sharp, tapered lines of my suit fit over me like a glove, the dark material soft against my skin and the burgundy pocket square providing a splash of color. For a firefighter, I had actually managed to clean up pretty well tonight. Not half bad if I did say so myself.

"Yeah, El. I think I am."

***

Xavier

As I made my way to the ceremony, Dexter by my side and standing in as my best man, the cool December air hit me, calming my nerves slightly. The garden was beautifully lit, with fairy lights twinkling in the trees and candles flickering along the path.

Our guests, coworkers from Station Twenty-One and their respective spouses and plus ones, were already seated, their faces turned expectantly toward the front. Even Jackson and his husband, Ayen, who sat staring at his husband in awe, tears shining behind his eyes, had flown out to Baton Rouge from California for our special day. The fact thrilled me to no end. I hadn't seen the man since I left my teaching position at the aerial program, the very program responsible for bringing Gage and I together, and moved to Baton Rouge three years ago. So much had happened for us both in that time and he looked good. Happy. Married life clearly agreed with him. A far cry from the player I'd known for most of my career there.

Kate and Dan were the other guests sitting in the second row that really shocked me. I'd invited them out of respect for Dexter but, truth be told, I never actually expected them to come. They'd been tolerant of my relationship with Gage, polite and cordial even whenever we had to interact in any way for something for our son, but I never actually expected them to support my impending nuptials on account of their religious morals. Color me impressed at Kate's changes over the last three years where my relationship with my son was concerned; she'd come leaps and bounds since that day I confronted her about the abuse our son had suffered. This though, sitting in actual support of me at my wedding, this was a change I could never have predicted. I knew having his mother there would mean the world to Dexter, too, and the thought that one day, despite our bad history, that Kate and I, and our respective spouses, might truly be a blended type of family for Dexter simply brought tears of happiness to my eyes. I wanted nothing more for my son than for all the past tensions and hurts to be erased and his future to be the brightest it could be. Maybe, just maybe, Kate's presence here today would be the start of that.

Captain Clarke stood at the front of the garden, an imposing yet welcoming figure. His navy dress uniform was immaculate, each medal and ribbon perfectly aligned. A tall man with broad shoulders and a dignified bearing, he commanded respect with a mere glance. His presence added a touch of formality and gravity to the occasion, but his warm smile and kind eyes softened his demeanor.

Captain Clarke had been a firefighter for over three decades, a Captain at Station Twenty-One, for the last one and a half, and his experience showed in the calm, steady way he carried himself. He had been a mentor to Gage, guiding him and supporting him through some of the toughest times in his career and his personal life, one of the very few commanders-in-chief who ran his station as an all inclusive, all accepting company, and it seemed only fitting that he would be the one to officiate our wedding.

I took my place at the front, standing tall and trying to steady my breathing even as I brushed at the tears collecting in the corners of my eyes. Dexter flashed me a smile and gave me a quick, one-armed hug, his supportive presence a comforting force.

He'd grown into such a fine young man, his grades at LSU were in the honorary role all through his last three years there, and amazingly, he'd gone to a therapist and managed to deal with all the horrors of his childhood and come out an incredible person despite that past. He'd even met someone he really liked and their relationship, though still in the early stages, seemed to add a sparkle to his eyes and a lightness to his step.

Our father/son relationship had progressed beyond my wildest expectations, and we often spent time together just doing things normal families did. All the things I'd missed out on in his childhood. I couldn't be more proud of the man he'd become, and I told him that often

The music started, and my heart skipped a beat. This was it.

As Gage appeared at the end of the aisle, my breath caught in my throat. He looked stunning, his smile lighting up the night. All the nerves, all the fear, melted away in that moment.

All I could see was him.

My love, my future.

When he reached me, we joined hands, and everything else faded into the background. It was just us, standing together, ready to face whatever came next. I squeezed his hands, and he squeezed mine back, his eyes shining with love.

"Ready?" he whispered, his voice

steady and sure.

"More than ever," I replied, my heart full to bursting.

And as we said our vows, surrounded by family and friends, I knew that this was just the beginning of our forever.

***

Gage

As Xavier and I joined hands and stood before him, Captain Clarke's deep voice resonated through the garden. "Ladies and gentlemen," he began, his gaze sweeping over the assembled guests, "we are gathered here today to celebrate the union of Gage and Xavier. It is an honor to stand before you, to witness and bless the commitment of these two remarkable men."

He paused, looking directly at us with a mix of pride and affection. "Gage, Xavier, you have chosen to walk this path together, to face the challenges and joys of life as partners joined in matrimony. Your love is a testament to your strength and your devotion to one another."

Standing just underneath a simple, yet elegant arch adorned with small white flowers, Captain Clarke's presence was both reassuring and inspiring. His words carried the weight of wisdom and experience, and as he continued the ceremony, I felt a sense of peace and certainty settle over me.

With Captain Clarke guiding us through our vows, just like he'd guided me through much of my life in the way that I thought a loving father would have, I knew we were in the best possible hands. His blessing was more than just ceremonial; it was a heartfelt endorsement from someone who had seen us grow and thrive together. Someone who I respected and cared for very much. His presence was a connection between our past and our future, and as we spoke the words that would bind us forever, his blessing falling over us, and the crowd cheering when we were pronounced husband and husband, I felt truly ready to take this next step in life with my man by my side.

Xavier was my heart, my everything.

He'd come into my lonely life and changed everything in ways I could in no way have imagined. My world would never be the same and I couldn't be more excited for our future together.

I pressed my lips to his when we were

finally granted the leave to do so, and with his hand grasped tightly in mine, tears of happiness tracing down my cheeks, we turned to face our family. As they all roared their approval, we made our way down the aisle together.

This was just how I'd dreamed my life would be.

One big family.

Thank you for reading the continuation of Xavier and Gage's story.

Oh, and if you enjoyed this book, maybe you'll consider doing me a huge favor and leaving a review. Even a few words would mean the world to me, and it also helps other readers find the stories you love.

XAVIER

Watch for Greyson, Asher, and Dexter to star in their own books sometime in the future. Don't forget to follow me on Facebook to keep up to date on all things yuMMy and the crazy antics of all the bad boys inside my head.

In the meantime, why not check out some of the other books in my backlist. A handy list is on the very next page! ☺

Love,

~Evie Riley

OTHER BOOKS BY EVIE

Federal Protection Agency
Mason
Rafe
Ryzen
Cooper
Noah
Damien
Sebastian
Gabe
Logan

Ruthless Empire
Courting Danger
Chasing Danger
Kissing Danger

Smokejumpers
Hawke
Cyrus
Jase
Gage
Jackson
Xavier

EVIE RILEY

Jasper Springs
Cade
Dawson
Drew
Grayson
Riley
Mitch

From The Edge
Shattered
Runaway
Jaded
Rescue
Hidden
Tormented

Gray Vale Pack
His Fated Mate
His Wounded Warrior
His Healing Heart

ABOUT THE AUTHOR

Evie Riley is a prolific, neurodivergent author known for her captivating MM romance novels. She has gained a significant following and topped the LGBT+ action and adventure bestseller charts with her series.

Evie's writing style often explores dark and gritty themes where her men must overcome difficult obstacles in their search for love, but she has also ventured into sweeter small-town romances, incorporating tropes like enemies-to-lovers, friends-to-lovers, age-gap, and forced proximity. She is known for crafting engaging romantic suspense novels and has a knack for creating interconnected series worlds that keep readers invested.

Interestingly, Ms. Riley has hinted at exploring new genres, such as Alien Omegaverse Romance, in the future.

Outside of writing, she enjoys spending time at the beach and has a quirky personality, described by her partner as ranging from cute to deadly, depending on her blood-chocolate levels.

Evie spends her nights writing bad boys in love, and her days wrangling the sweet boys she loves.